Praise for

"Haunting, nuanced, and h[...]sential reading. Lemberg ref[...] away from the hurt we can do to one another, while reminding us that through listening, labor, and mutual support, we can reject patterns of harm and cultivate something better. In these hard times, *Yoke of Stars* feels as necessary as air, as water, as kindness."
—Izzy Wasserstein, author of *These Fragile Graces, This Fugitive Heart*

"This is a story about trauma and strife and magic, of stars that hold and bind and devour, and maybe, just maybe, it's about the possibility of something else beyond the hurt and pain. The way the stories in the book touch and interweave, the way the characters in them tug and pull at each other, is beautifully done—and I love how deftly Lemberg pulls all the threads together into a complex, striking weave."
—Maria Haskins, author of *Wolves and Girls*

"For fellow word-nerds, Lemberg's linguistic explorations are a thought-provoking journey into how language influences all of us. Lemberg's command of language and narrative nuance makes this a haunting, beautiful read."
—Marian Crane, author of the *Lonhra Sequence*

"R. B. Lemberg's Birdverse is one of fantasy's most immersive, lyrical, and mind-expanding universes, to which this dream of a novella adds dazzling new depths. *Yoke*

of Stars is a beautiful tale about the stories we all live within, about the languages and connections that bind us to each other and trap us within the same."
—Jason Sanford, author of *Plague Birds*

"When I tell you that this book essentially altered my neural pathways, I mean that in so many good ways. Everything about this book, from the writing, the imagery, the character development, the world building, is just luminous. A gorgeous, lush, super queer fantasy."
—Wulfe Wulfemeyer, The Raven Book Store

Praise for *The Unbalancing*

"The lush lyricism of the mythology, culture, and history in *The Unbalancing* is illustrious and transportive. It's an enchanting world of star lore, magic, and gender identity with a roster of heartfelt characters told with such rich prose that kept me rooting for Ranra."
—Tlotlo Tsamaase, *The Silence of the Wilting Skin*

"R. B. Lemberg's Birdverse is one of my favorite places to visit, full of queer possibilities and deep emotional and philosophical musings. In *The Unbalancing*, they give us wonder, devastation, resilience, and love."
—Julia Rios, Hugo Award–winning editor of *Uncanny Magazine*

"*The Unbalancing* is a story of people and their power, in nature and society, in interactions and relationships, and

of consent and belonging, and of failure and hope."
—Scott H. Andrews, World Fantasy Award–winning editor/publisher of *Beneath Ceaseless Skies*

Praise for *The Four Profound Weaves*

★"Nebula-nominated Lemberg's first novella, set in their deeply queer 'Birdverse' universe, presents a beautiful, heartfelt story of change, family, identity, and courage. Centering two older transgender protagonists in the midst of emotional and physical journeys highlights the deep, meaningful prose that Lemberg always brings to their stories."
—*Library Journal*, starred review

"Thoughtful and deeply moving, *The Four Profound Weaves* is the anti-authoritarian, queer-mystical fairy tale we need right now."
—Annalee Newitz, author of *Autonomous* and *The Future of Another Timeline*

★"Lemberg writes deeply considered, evocative portraits of their characters, handling sexuality and gender especially well. This diverse, folkloric fantasy world is a delight to visit."
—*Publishers Weekly*, starred review

★"Impressive world building renders the shifting hues of the desert sands and the cold stone of The Collector's palace in tight prose."
—*Foreword*, starred review

Yoke of Stars

Copyright © 2024 by R. B. Lemberg

Interior and cover design by Elizabeth Story
Author photo by Bogi Takács

Tachyon Publications LLC
1459 18th Street #139
San Francisco, CA 94107
415.285.5615
www.tachyonpublications.com
tachyon@tachyonpublications.com

Series editor: Jacob Weisman
Editor: Jaymee Goh

Print ISBN: 978-1-61696-418-4
Digital ISBN: 978-1-61696-419-1

Printed in the United States by Versa Press, Inc.

First Edition: 2024
9 8 7 6 5 4 3 2 1

R.B. LEMBERG

YOKE OF STARS

A BIRDVERSE BOOK

TACHYON • SAN FRANCISCO

Also by R. B. Lemberg

Marginalia to Stone Bird (2016)
The Four Profound Weaves (2020)
Geometries of Belonging (2022)
The Unbalancing (2022)
Everything Thaws (2023)

As Editor:
Here, We Cross: a collection of queer and genderfluid poetry from Stone Telling 1 – 7 (2012)
An Alphabet of Embers (2016)

For the exiles and the translators

I.
DOWNWARD

IN THE BEGINNING, Bird brought us the stars.

There were twelve of them, each of different color—twelve triumphant stars that sang in the tail of the goddess as she descended toward the newborn land. Down there, in the scorching heart of the desert, the first guardians sang and danced as the goddess swooped closer, and Bird danced with them, and one by one the stars fell down from her tail. Each guardian caught a falling star, and later they planted the stars in their many homelands. From these buried stars, magic was born: deepnames shining like seeds of light in the earth, and in people's minds. And these great buried stars have guarded the land since then; they guard it even now.

It's a common story, I think. I learned it here, in the desert. But there is more than one way to tell about the Birdcoming. Each tradition is different—some very different.

Here is the story I learned long ago. I, Stone Orphan of the siltway people, translate it now into your language.

The goddess Bird was nearing her destination when the Star of the Shoal began to remember itself. The past was dangerous, so the star would allow itself to remember only what was useful for its survival.

More was needed now. Having recalled just enough to re-form a consciousness, the Star of the Shoal looked inward, where shimmering, fishlike nodes came together in a whirligig of silver—scales and shards of light. Sea-minnows they were, and also souls, souls of the dead who made up the star. Magical deepnames flared within some of the minnows, and others were magicless, but all were bonded together—soul to soul, deepname to deepname. Those without magic were held by magic extended from others, forming a collective which was the Star of the Shoal.

Eleven other stars clung to the streaming tail of the goddess, and they were so different. There were no souls inside that the Star of the Shoal could discern. Only deepnames, brighter and stronger at the core and wispier and longer at the outer tendrils. People are needed to give birth to deepnames, but only the magic survived.

But what about those without magic? Were they abandoned?

The Star of the Shoal shuddered with the repulsive strangeness of it, examining itself once more, tracking each soul-minnow and every bond just to make sure of its people. Some were missing, indeed, but most were accounted for, each soul a part of a generation extending in a horizontal plane and connecting vertically to generations below and above.

All dead, something deep within it suggested.

Death has no meaning within the collective of the Bonded Shoal, something else within it supplied. *Bodies are always temporary.*

Shhh, whispered another voice. This one was soft and at the same time wise, and it carried in it a melody which was immaterial and endless like the void. This voice sang, *Attend now.*

Bird was descending.

Through the outer layers of the sky the goddess plunged, her tail streaming behind her. The air around her was multicolored, a melody wrapping around her like an embrace that guided her gently down toward the newly formed world.

Not much could be seen from above but for the parting of clouds, and the clear skies below. The rainbow of music surrounding Bird dissolved into the air. Some moments later, music rose from a place of sand, to greet the descending Bird and the stars she was bringing.

A dozen people swayed and sang and played instruments, reveling in the dance of the goddess, the great Birdcoming. And oh, how she danced, her tail as wide as the sky and as narrow as shards, swirling and diving and circling through the air above the desert and its dancers. One by one, the people there lifted their hands toward Bird, and one by one, the stars fell from her tail, each singing or humming softly in anticipation of being caught.

The Star of the Shoal edged farther away from its jubilant fellows, and began to discourse with itself.

These dancing guardians are untrustworthy, said something within it.

These are nameway and dreamway. We've had such neighbors before, echoed another.

They won't understand us, let alone safeguard us.

They will trick us and trap us. Betray us, just like before.

Look, said another. A wistful voice, strong and young. *There's a serious one—here he is.* And indeed, below, the Star of the Shoal noticed a person who stood apart from the others. He held no musical instruments, and neither did he dance, but looking at him, the Star of the Shoal perceived more than heard a powerful voice, a song the color of red, that beckoned and guided it.

Come to me.

This man was strong in the body, but bodies were unimportant. His soul, though, would be a powerful anchor; he could form many bonds with others, and never loosen his grip. The name of this man was Ladder.

We should fall into his hands, said a voice within the Star of the Shoal. *He will catch us and hold us, even though he is nameway.*

He knows what it is like to be orphaned, another voice said.

We won't let ourselves fall into any one hand, said another, an ancient-sounding voice. *We are the collective. We are the Bonded Shoal.*

Another one like it echoed, *The Shoal shall have no masters, no teachers, no leaders, no guides. The Shoal shall have no keepers, no guards. No jailers.*

The Shoal will not fall in again with the nameway and dreamway.

The Shoal will survive alone, or else it is not to survive, added another.

The wistful voice said, *The Shoal has no masters, but we are already carried by Bird. We are already delivered by someone.*

All the more reason to fall on our own, and as fast as we can, echoed many. *So we can be free.*

The Star of the Shoal attended to the many soul-minnows within it. Seventy generations in a fluid, undulating, layered collective. Each soul was now examined, accounted for, counted.

Those who wish to fall into these hands are outnumbered, said the Star of the Shoal to itself. *We fall alone, as quickly as we can. We fall into a body of water.*

Seventy generations of soul-minnows now looked down to the ground, and began calculating their path. The Star of the Shoal started to buzz, shimmering silver in Bird's vision, confusing the goddess until her dance became more erratic. Her tail elongated beyond the horizon, swinging and swaying over the whole of the land.

Now, ancient and young voices spoke in the Shoal. *Now, now, now, now.*

Below, on the ground, the starkeeper known as Ladder raised his hands and called for the Star of the Shoal to come to him, but it streaked through the sky, falling and falling and falling into the cold expanses of the unnamed northern sea.

Into the icy water it plunged, dissolving for a moment, each soul shining in the darkness like a small, silvery sea-minnow. Then, in another moment, the shoal reformed. The bonds between souls, darkened by impact, flared into light once again.

The seawater was deep, and within it the Star of the

Shoal now floated, attending to itself.

We can stay here, below, said the ancient voices. *Nobody will see us. We will continue our existence.*

We must rise, and graze the surface. Some of us must take bodies and live.

If we take bodies, said other voices, *they will need to be fed and clothed and kept. We will need resources, and those can be lost or taken away. It is better to be underwave.*

The Star of the Shoal remembered some more of what was useful for it to remember. *Carried by Bird as she passed through the void that lies between the worlds,* it said, *we lost many souls on the outer layers. Much as we rotated and reformed to protect all within the collective, some were exposed more than others, and perished. The damage extends deep and wide, into at least seven generations from the outermost layers, and this now needs to be repaired, regrown. Even without this damage, the Shoal cannot continue to survive for long without the nourishment of the living. Some of us must acquire bodies and live, so that they die and become ancestors.*

The soul-minnows attended to the voice of the Shoal.

The lower layers of the Bonded Shoal now sank deeper, reaching the bottom of the northern sea. Slowly, over many years, the soul-minnows moved pebbles and began to push them toward the surface. In a hundred years, a small island rose. In the next hundred years, another.

Seven isles were pushed to the surface this way, and were allowed to grow thick with moss. This land could now be, perhaps, habitable by those who wished to take bodies.

Dead, something within the Star of the Shoal said. *All dead.*

Then live again for a short while, encouraged the Star of the Shoal. *Fulfill your duty to the collective. Rise and multiply.*

Heeding the voice of their star, seven minnows detached from the sunken Shoal and swam toward the surface, each choosing an isle for itself. When they emerged onto the land, they had the looks of people— silvery-skinned and lustrous, with round fish eyes on the sides of the face. They were all named strong, all with multiple deepnames. Some of these deepnames connected to the Shoal of ancestors below. And now the seven extended their unattached deepnames toward each other, bonding themselves into a new generation.

"We are siltway," sang one of them from an isle, a rounded, short person with a lilting and powerful voice. "I form a storyline, and call it Song."

"We are siltway," spoke a firm, strong voice from another isle. "I too form a storyline, and call it Stone."

One by one, the namers of the new storylines announced themselves: Song, Stone, Fish, Moss, Feeder, Boater, and Weaver.

Hearing this reckoning, new soul-minnows arose from the water, separating from the Shoal with its ancestral minnow-souls to join the generation that lived again, for a short while. Each of these souls joined a storyline, preparing to do the labor of singing and feeding and fishing, the growing of moss, and weaving it into clothes, and shaping the stone. This work would build the siltway isles and maintain them. The newly formed

siltway people would birth children to continue the storylines. The children formed new bonds between themselves and their parents, and between themselves and
their own generation. When the in-between generation
died in the body, the bonds extended once more between
living and the dead.

The Bonded Shoal existed again, as it had elsewhere,
before. A powerful body of star with its dead—the souls
in the sea, connected to each other through the magic
of bonds; and above the submerged Star of the Shoal,
the shallow layer of a living generation. They were much
diminished, but they had survived the journey through
the void.

All was, once again, as it should be.

But in the depths of the Star of the Shoal lived a
memory of a man called Ladder. The Star itself had forgotten him, remembering only what was useful to its
survival. But deep within it, the souls that had been
overruled by the collective still remembered, and remembering, heard the voice of his song.

II.
AWAY FROM

I LIVE IN THE THIRD TERRACE NOW, where assassin-trainees spend their final circle of training. This part of our training is to be still. To listen. To wait for the first real client to take a chance on my skill. If the assassination succeeds, I will graduate, but until then, I must stay here. In this land, the land of the nameway, I learned about *verbs*, about *movement* upon *ground*—but all I do is sit in a room with almost no water. There is a small pool for me, in the corner. I can almost feel the water evaporate into the desert air, drop by drop, leaving only salt. My gills are painfully dry. I am still.

I wait for a month for someone to come. Then I wait even longer.

It is noon, and someone is climbing up the sandstone stairs. I hope for a client, but anyone will do after six weeks of sitting.

I listen to the sounds and attend. The visitor's steps are noisy and unguarded. Their body's heat is wrapped in the incessant heat of the sun-streaked air. It must be a client. Please.

They climb to the top of the third terrace and stop.

I am desperate, not that I'd show it. Still, my lips

move, and sounds emerge from my mouth. "Come in."

It is still so strange to attend to the movement of lips. To notice the body. Even the way I think keeps changing, flickering between the language of the desert and my old siltway speech. I already think too much in the nameway tongue. So many verbs. Soon I will be without my birth words, and it feels . . . strange—not grief-like, not peace-like, though perhaps both, flaring and subsiding like the magic of my deepnames.

"Come in," I say again, louder.

"Thank you." The newcomer's voice is resonant and deep, and pleasant to hear. Shadows are slanting against the round opening to my room. In this final circle of training, we do not get a door.

A person comes in. They are nameway. They are of medium build, somewhat taller than me, and dressed in dun-colored traveling clothes, plain but clearly well-made. Their skin is olive-brown, lighter than the desert nameway. The newcomer's long, dark hair is braided into a single braid. They are young. No, old.

I swear at myself—still, after all this training and time, I can't tell the nameway apart.

I strain my senses, squinting the way the Headmaster taught me, to see the visitor as a body I can kill.

They are about thirty.

They remind me of someone, but most nameway people look alike to me.

I am distraught, and I do not understand why. So I make a movement with my hand, motioning to the bare sandstone floor. "Will you sit with me?" I ask.

"Gladly." The person's face is in shadow. It is bright

outside, but my room is dim. I wonder if they really are glad, or if this is a quirk of nameway speech—to lie. I never learned how to do this, either; I can only keep silent.

They sit down. Perhaps they would want coverlets or cushions. Other assassin-trainees acquire them, but I see no need for such things. Except now I feel strange, as if I have broken a rule. Nameway people like soft things. This person has no carpet with them, just a small bag.

I speak over my hesitations. "I am called Stone Orphan."

"I am Ulín."

"Ou-leen?" I drag out the vowels, knowing that I am misspeaking. My lips move, and it is a strain to notice them.

They do not seem upset. "Ulín. Short vowels—first, you draw the corners of your lips together for a short ou. Then, the stress on the short ee. Ulín."

I repeat, and get closer this time.

I say, "I have not thought before how the corners of my lips can shape sounds."

"All sounds can be described that way." Ulín's face lights up, animated by excitement. "Most vowels are about the tongue and the lips. Is your tongue up at the roof of your mouth? Is it down? Is the shape of your lips rounded? And so on. If you want, I can say more."

I understand, with sudden clarity, that this is technical knowledge, like the skills of the body and the blade I learned here. This person reminds me of someone, yes—of my elder Old Song—and my heart catches.

I want to say, *Yes, teach me.*

Instead, I go for the center of things. "You must have

come here to purchase an assassination. So name your target, and let us come to terms."

"Wait," Ulín says. "Please. May I ask why you're here?"

I blink. "I am here to kill your target."

"No—" Ulín says. "I mean, you are siltway . . ."

I try not to recoil. And to think I liked her—them— enjoyed the sound of their voice—they reminded me of Old Song. But this person is not my elder. They are some random nameway, a client, as callous and terrible as the rest.

I do not want to be angry, but it happens regardless. "I am an assassin, and this is the School of Assassins. Where else would you want me to be?" Nowhere, not to exist? *Call me fish already and let's get this over with. It's how you people know about us anyway. Fish stories from a remote land. Fairytales about the world's strange places.*

"I'm so sorry," the visitor says. And here it is again, the soft, deep voice. Their hands spread on their knees where I can see them. "It's my fault. I was startled to see a siltway person in the Great Burri Desert, and I wondered about your water . . . It was wrong of me. Please forgive me. Anybody can be anywhere."

Ulín surprises me. Their words are the ebb and flow of the tide. But I am still angry.

"Anybody can be anywhere," I echo. "That's right." But all of my people are elsewhere, and I am far from the sea. I explain, needlessly. "There in the corner—it's a shallow pool of water mixed with salt. At night, I immerse in it to sleep." If the Headmaster heard me blather so, he'd fail me all the way back to second circle. Maybe even the first. "Anything else you want to know?"

Ulín smiles. It is so open, warm, and their eyes are shining again. "I want to learn your language."

"What?"

"I am a language scholar."

I don't think anybody had smiled at me like this before. I am confused by Ulín, confused how they use feminine forms when they speak Burrashti, how much they—she—they, I cannot be sure—how much Ulín reminds me of Old Song. A younger Old Song. Burrashti is not their native tongue, I remind myself—neither is it mine.

I ask, cautious not to reveal my turmoil. "What is a language scholar?"

Ulín says, "I like to learn about languages which are not my own. It is important to me to understand another person in their own language. To learn a language, one must change oneself. I value that."

Now the whole thing does not make sense to me. "You have come all this way to the School of Assassins." To the court of sandstone terraces Ladder has built above the buried Orphan Star. "You must have exerted your body for months just to get here. To the desert, where there are no siltway. All this to ask *me* about *my language?*"

"No." Ulín lowers her head. "No, you're right, I had no idea you'd be here. To tell you the truth, I came here because I heard the song. It was a melody of red that beckoned and summoned me."

This makes no sense, either. "All would-be assassins hear this melody," I say. "I heard it too. Have you been accepted to train?"

"No!" Ulín is startled. I want to know if Ulín is a woman like Old Song, or if I am mistaken. Should I use the language of they or the language of she? Perhaps something yet different? It shouldn't matter. I just need to graduate.

I say, "I am trying to understand. You are here for some reason. What for, if not to train or to hire?"

Ulín's voice is sad now. A sound like dusk, like the surf striking stone. "I did come to purchase an assassination, I'm just not sure about the target. The Headmaster thought you could help me."

Not sure about the target. "More than one person harmed you." It is not a question.

Ulín does not look at me. "Not . . . at the same time."

"May I ask," I say. "Are you a woman? Forgive me."

"Oh yes," she says. "And you?"

"I've been told I'm a woman, too."

She nods at me, warm, and I think that I want to help her. This has been the strangest of conversations, but I missed this. Talking. Just being with another person, even a nameway.

"How about we trade stories?" I say. I'd had this arrangement with someone before, someone who looked a bit like her, but it's hard for me to distinguish between nameway. "Let's exchange a story for a story. That's fair."

"Mine are painful," she says, grimacing.

"That's what stories are," I say. Old Song taught me that. "Stories are yearning and pain."

Ulín gulps. "Forgive me—I am not sure that's all that stories can be. But mine—" She turns her head halfway toward the light. There is something strange going on with her head, her magic, but I am not ready to pry.

She says, "I am sorry to ask but . . . would you mind starting first? Tell me how you came to learn Burrashti." I blink, and she explains, "Burrashti is the name of the language of the desert. We are speaking it now. It is not my first language either, forgive me. So my words are simple."

"It's fine," I say. Fine is not the right word for this feeling, but I don't know how to name it. We are both strangers here, speaking a language not our own. But Ulín is nameway, so for her another nameway language is just different-sounding words. *I* had to twist my whole being into a new shape to learn to speak like the nameway do, and now I cannot become untwisted.

I explain, "When I spoke my own language, I could not imagine how your people lived. Learning your language, being able to speak it means that I myself changed. Now I don't understand how my own people live."

"Because your language has no verbs." Ulín's eyes are bright, but I do not know how she knows this, and it alarms me.

"I first learned this from a book," she explains. "It endlessly fascinated me, but I could not figure out how it works. A language with no verbs."

I sigh. "We mark directions. Up, above, down, across, back, forward, sideways. Directions are bonds between words."

"There's more to it." Ulín is smiling, but I do not know why she is happy.

I say, "My people don't move like you do. We flicker, siltway soul from siltway soul, one bonded person to

19

another. Up, above, down, across, back, forward, sideways, into the deep. Even the stones of our isles are not fixed in place—they are floated, supported by a net of soul-bonds. Alive or dead, we are bonded in the Shoal." It does not make me happy to explain it, or to think about it.

Ulín nods, her face is serious now, matching my mood. "And do you still . . . flicker, Stone Orphan?"

My shoulder twitches. I school my features into assassin smoothness, throttling any visible trace of bitterness. "I use my feet. I *walk*. I *speak*, using verbs."

She struggles, I can see, maybe guessing that I am struggling, but in the end she cannot stop herself. She is curious, and this reminds me of myself, before I came here.

"Forgive me, Stone Orphan . . . Do you translate then, in your mind? I find that translation is a kind of bridge for words."

"I do not know this word."

"A bridge," she says, "is a structure built over a body of water, so that people can cross."

I snap, finally. "What people? *My* people have no use for such structures."

Ulín looks distressed at my reaction, and ashamed, and I take pity on her. "I think that translation is a departure. A pushing-away-from. One is trying to leave. And arrival is always uncertain."

A story of yearning

I yearned, see. This feeling that nameway people express with a verb. But you nameway do not mark the direction of yearning, leaving it meaningless, floundering. My yearning came from below, from the deep-down where the souls of the ancestors were. I heard a song of red that reached me from the depths, surfacing through countless generations, and it beckoned to me and disturbed me.

I am of the Stone storyline. Song people sing our stories, reminding us of who we are; Fish people catch the fish; and Moss people maintain the moss which the Feeder people make into food to sustain our bodies. Weaver people make some of the moss into garments to warm us in the cold, long winters. Each storyline has a purpose, but Stone is barely needed now. Seventy-six generations ago, when the ancestors lifted the isles, the Stone storyline was tasked with chiseling shallow dwellings in the newly surfaced rock for all of us, so that we could find shelter there. Dwellings that would hold water to let us breathe easy when we sank down to sleep, and dwellings that let us surface and inhale the air when we awoke.

Ulín interrupts me to speak. "I myself used to live underwater."

I ask, "How would you, a nameway, live underwater? You do not have a siltway body—and I have not heard—"

She whispers, "Among the dreamway."

I am not sure I understand, and I am confused, but she shakes her head. "I will tell you my story when yours is done."

I say, "All right . . . Where was I? Yes—the Stone storyline."

Long ago, the purpose of people within our storyline was to fashion dwellings out of the body of stone. But that purpose was exhausted long ago. It existed for one generation only.

What, then, was the purpose of Stone? What was our labor, beyond helping the other storylines and being diminished with each generation? I worried about it as I lay in the shallow stone cavern fashioned by my ancestors, generations ago. I lay in darkness, breathing the tide, my body sinking deeper into the watery pool of the bed. My eyes closed. I called on the magic of my two deepnames, and with their power extended, I saw a glittering web. The bonds spooled out of me like moss-yarn in water, showing me how I was tied to my people. Among the living I was bonded to Old Song, an elder of the Song storyline, who was at that time on an island quite a distance away from my dwelling. And among the dead I was bonded to the one who birthed me. My *mother*, a nameway would say, but we do not mark these genders, and so we do not have these words like the nameway do.

Through the one that birthed me, who also had two deepnames, I was connected to many generations deepening into the Shoal. Through my bond with Old Song, who had three deepnames, I was connected to the living and dead souls of Song, Moss, Stone, and Weaver storylines, and through these souls to every one of us, making up a star.

The Star of the Shoal flared in my sleepy vision, shining gently underwater—ancestor souls like slim, silvery fish waving in a gentle current, whole undulating woven sheets of them, and above them a slim shining layer of us, of the living.

This is how I would fall asleep every night. But this time, through my connection to Old Song that led me back to the oldest of Stone, I perceived a glimmer of red.

Ulín asks, "What happens to those without deepnames, if they cannot bond?" Her voice is curious, a bit broken. I was taught to listen to such things.

I say, "Oh, they bond. Those without magic are held by the others. They are mortar." As I speak, I watch Ulín's face, the minute changes in it—pain, regret. Resignation.

23

How did I not notice this before? I speak again. "You, yourself, have no deepnames." It is not a question.

Ulín's face goes pale, and I notice things, just as the Headmaster taught me; I notice what should have been obvious if I paid better attention. "I should have noticed before—you are magicless—and yet, you are not mortar. Your deepnames have been torn from you by violence!"

She turns her face away from me. This, this is why she is here. This is a great crime, a terrible misfortune. Someone must pay, and I will gladly collect. "So you're here to purchase a contract on your assailant."

"Please," she says. "Please stop."

I, too, am too curious for my own good. It was silly of me to think that part of me ended. "Forgive me, Ulín. I just wanted to understand."

She does not answer. I have pried too much, and she has pried too much, but I do not want her to be silent. I want her to ask me questions and I want to ask her, too.

The silence weighs me down until I blurt out, "You're different from other clients. You do not call me a fish under your breath, you do not look away from my face."

She frowns. "Why would I?"

"Even Ladder thought I was strange, before he trained me and steeled himself to my appearance."

She speaks quietly. "I think you're wonderful, Stone Orphan."

Her words grate on me. This word, *wonderful*, it does not belong here. "You want something," I say. "I already said I'll consider your contract. No need to flatter me."

"I'm probably here to purchase a contract. But mostly,

I am trying to understand." Ulín closes her eyes and begins to speak smoothly and slowly in the language of the desert. She speaks as if she is singing. "This is something I always want—something that brings me to ruin and yet this something is mine—not simple curiosity, but a thirst for deep knowledge, a joy in the shape and branching of it. I want to know how language is formed between people, how language precedes and survives us. I think—I believe—I know that language is a living creature that changes and writhes between us, that ascends from the ancestors and rises through us toward all the future people who wait, yet unborn, to speak it . . ."

I say, "Your words are beautiful. I do not fully grasp them." She reminds me so much of Old Song that I feel my eyes stinging. "Let me tell you about Old Song."

That deep melody bothered and beckoned me every night. In my language, it was an undulation of wave, moonless and restless, a scrape of odd weather from strange and unbonded corners. I was disturbed. In the isles, one does not pay that much attention to oneself. But a single person's unease can disrupt the whole Shoal. We can commit crimes by yearning, I think. Yearning for a different way, for knowledge perhaps, but really for danger.

When a soul darts aside, like a bright and terrified fish, it can drag the whole shoal with it toward danger. Straying endangers all—and so we must give any bad feelings away to a wise one from the Song storyline. A Song person will first understand it, then sing it, then diffuse it in water and weather. After that, again we become calm.

Old Song was my bonded through my strongest deepname, the one with a single syllable. Before we were bonded, Old Song sought me out. They were old and large, the silver-gray of their face darkened with age into a color of the evening sea. Faded scales, almost white and pearlescent, covered the sides of their face, and their fin-hair was limp. Their eyes were faded, too, into a very pale blue. I later learned that they had a different name once, but I was never told what it was.

"In myself," Old Song said, "there is a deepname that once was a two-syllable. It has recently been shortened. It is now stronger and has one syllable. The bond which attached to my two-syllable is no more. You are young and have an unattached deepname, also with one syllable. Will you bond with me?"

It was strange to hear about Old Song's destroyed bond. Such things do not happen among us. We are all bonded forever.

"Your bonded person died?" I asked, but it could not be right. We remain bonded after we die. Once the body dies, the deepname structure that contains our souls simply sinks undersea. The bonds do not break once we become ancestors.

"Not died," Old Song said. "The bond itself was destroyed."

I was terrified, and flattered to be asked to bond with an elder, but I could not stop asking questions. "So what happened to the person you were bonded to, when the bond was destroyed?"

Old Song's light-blue eyes deepened to storm. "They are gone."

This conversation felt like a sliver of ice in my mouth. Strange and exhilarating and blood-in-my-cheeks sharp. "Why do you want my bond?"

"Because you are strong," Old Song said. "I need you to anchor to the pain I carry. To keep me in place. This is, after all, the forgotten purpose of Stones. Before the Star of the Shoal was carried on Bird's tail, Stones were warriors."

"Warriors?" I tasted that unfamiliar word in my mouth. *Kahren*. In our language, it sounded almost like *kahir*. *Stone*.

"Those strong in the body, those who protect the Shoal," said Old Song. "Strong and curious are Stone and Song, and so we are matched. We are the foundational storylines. You will anchor me here, in the isles."

But I am curious too, I wanted to say. Instead I bit my tongue bloody, attuning me further to the world's presence, the rock upon which I perched, the woven garment of moss on my body, at times chafing and comforting. I felt the tiny drops of seawater hitting my skin as the wave crashed ceaselessly against Stone Isle, the salt on my tongue, the smell of seaweed and some unfamiliar spice wafting from Old Song's moss-woven garment. It was centering, calming; I could close my eyes tightly and drift into sleep until Old Song flickered away.

But my eyes remained open.

After a while I noticed that Old Song waded in water, their feet not quite touching Stone Isle. How did they come here? Did they flicker to me, or to someone else among the Stones? Or did they, perhaps, cover the distance in some other, different, more laborious way? I wondered if they would tell me anything at all if I simply waited. It would be good to wait, to stay suspended between the sea and the sky, to wait for an understanding.

But I was restless, so I asked, "Why is Stone the second most important storyline?"

Old Song's mouth moved, but the words I heard reverberated only in my mind. *"Because Stone supports the Song that must issue forth, for us to exist and continue. Without Song, we leave no trace, we disappear. Without Stone, we cannot be protected, cannot be anchored, we drift and we drift apart. I cannot let myself drift. My song must be here."*

I wanted to know more, but I knew that we came close to bonding already, Old Song's words in my mind, the feeling of them in my bones. It was as intimate as sharing bodies would be, but through stories—like two waves coming together, water and water distinguished by nothing but the primeval force that pushes both waves to meet and merge. I could resist this. Cast my mind elsewhere. But already I learned from Old Song, and the desire for more was a tidal pull. Bodies were unimportant. When my body died, I would still be bonded to this elder, still a part of their song.

"Kah," I said. My single-syllable deepname.

Ulín gasps, and I feel the corners of my mouth twitch up. "You are surprised I utter my deepname in your presence?"

"This is not done. It is dangerous to share—"

I shrug. "What would you do with it? You are nameless. You have suffered nameloss. Did you give your deepnames out to strangers?"

She shakes her head. "No."

"Of course not," I say. "Whoever did this to you did not know your deepnames, and yet they harmed you."

Ulín swallows, about to protest something, but then she looks away. What did I even say? Ah. Perhaps it wasn't a stranger. I say, "You *did* give your deepnames to someone?"

"No, no," Ulín says. "It doesn't matter."

"But . . . it wasn't a stranger."

Ulín nods, speechless.

"A loved one. Of course." Why else would she hesitate, having come all this way, to name her target and bargain with me for a contract? I do not want to say, but it usually is a loved one. Especially for women.

I tell her, "I belong with the Orphan Star now. If I decide to take your commission, I'll kill the one you want me to kill. They, too, will feed the Orphan Star. Many students come to this court and are killed here in training, and those who survive to graduate accept contracts and kill. All these perished souls are devoured by the Orphan. This is the true cost of the contract, the heart of all that happens here. The knowledge of my deepname will not serve you."

"I'm sorry," she says.

"For what?"

Ulín replies, "For interrupting your story. For implying you did not know what you were doing."

Her words do something to me, warm and sharp and hard to define. "I accept your apology."

"Thank you," she murmurs. "I want to know more. I want to learn more words. Could you teach me the siltway words for toward, and below, and across?"

"Why would you want them? To speak like we do? You cannot. This is a translation. I translate and I am translated, and so you will only translate these echoes." The story I tell will move further and further away from the Shoal. What will remain, once the story is moved all the way to Ulín's side? Untruths. An echo of that old feeling. To exhale mist, to inhale vapor. In and out with the tension of breath.

"I spoke and spoke," I say. "I want to hear your story now."

She gulps. I see her throat move. "It is a story of despair."

"Listen," I tell her. "It is not wrong or shameful to despair. This is the deepest meaning of the Orphan Star. It feeds on our despair, and those disdained by the world will always have a place inside it." All over the land people flee from despair, deny it exists, seek to silence it. Except here. People, yes: nameway and dreamway and siltway alike. Most are afraid to acknowledge the power and pull of despair. But those who do, come here, and they are embraced by the vast Orphan Star that lies underground, and become a part of its shining.

"So tell me your story, Ulín. Please."

A story of pain

There was a tall stone house on a shore, built by Ulín's ancestor Ranra when she arrived to the Coast in her ships, steering her people away from disaster. This ancestral home was called Ranra's Towers. It was built of gray stone and embraced by thick vines, like lichen with leaves climbing from its foundational boulders to the very top of the outlook, so that the Coastal people could gaze at the sea. To the west was a beach of fine sand—like the desert, but colder, and swept by the wave.

When the tide receded, Ulín would go there to look for shells. The shells had once housed small sea creatures, mollusks and crabs that had joined their ancestors, leaving their houses for her curious fingers to find. When she put a conch to her ear, she heard the eternal and restless voice of the sea.

It is there that Ulín saw the prince.

He had a long body of glistening green, with fins of saltwater. He moved effortlessly in the wave, like a language that promised new meanings that she did not yet know. His three companions—smaller than him but also illustrious—followed him in the wave. Since that day Ulín would spy on them, gazing from afar at their games. She observed them from the crumbled outlook atop Ranra's Towers.

She would hide behind rocks on a beach, curious and charmed, until one day the serpents stepped onto the shore in the bodies of young men with long hair of braided seaweed and shell.

They were the dreamway people of the serpent, who lived in the sea, not far from the shore. The dreamway magic is different from the magic of deepnames. Those with the strongest magic were shapechangers. One shape was human; another that of a sea-serpent, attained through the mastery of the dreaming sea which stretches wide and vast above the waking lands. In those dreaming wilds, neither the nameway nor the siltway people would venture. And *he* was a prince of his people, a shape-changer powerful in the domains of waking and dream. Ulín's people and his were enemies once. In the past.

Ulín wanted to befriend him, and so she resolved to learn his language. How else would she know him? How else to know anything? Language is the gleaming heart of all things—for nameway, and siltway, and dreamway. When Bird brought the stars to the land, she must have brought language, too.

When Ulín walked toward the youths of the serpent people, her younger sibling—her brother—observed from the shadows. She did not know it, at first.

Again and again, Ulín would go out in secret to meet her sea-serpent prince, with his eyes of emerald green, and his hair of seaweed braided with carved bone. His name was Laufkariar. Like a caress of the wave. He wanted her to come with him, to visit his realm under the sea.

It is not easy for a nameway person to breathe underwater, but Ulín had powerful magic back then. Two deepnames, like two stars in her mind, an explosion of pain and power. This structure is known among the nameway as the Princely Angle, a combination of two deepnames, a single-syllable and a two-syllable; its magic is that of adventure and daring.

And so Ulín called on the power of her deepnames, and created for herself a bubble of breath. It would not last forever. Just a few hours. But Laufkariar wanted to show her life in his palace under the tide. There was a dreamway city beneath the serpent-shaped gate of ivory and emerald that juts out of the sea, dividing the expanse of the water between the ancient, lost Sinking Lands and Ulín's homeland, the Coast. A long time ago her ancestor Ranra had been allowed to lead her ships through that gate, at a price of betrayal. Ulín wanted to know the serpent side of that story more even than she wanted his embrace. She wanted words—words themselves—the sounds and meanings they make, and the shapes of them strung together. It is beautiful, she thought, to know that languages live in their people like serpents that molt and change shape in each generation, regrowing new words and new sounds, and people are simply the carriers, the many-breathed bodies of it. She wanted to carry that serpent of the tongue, to possess all treasures which shine only when they are clothed in gesture or sound.

I interrupt Ulín, and my voice is raw. "You are a poet. Do you sing?"

She shakes her head. "I am not creative."

I do not believe her for a moment. "Do you at least translate?"

Ulín nods. "Sure, but I am not much of a translator. That is not why I learn languages."

"Why, then?" Why would anyone do it unless they had to?

"I want to carry multiple languages within me, feel them writhe and entwine in my mind. It is the best thing."

"It is not." I will be calm. Calm. "Carrying two languages at the same time is, it is . . ." I will my voice not to grate, not to break. "It is a departure without an arrival. It is a strangeness that makes you aware, but does not let you simply be. Your thoughts forever reflect back, fractured."

"I do not see it this way," she begins. Then says, "I am sorry. Perhaps your story is very different from mine."

I tell Ulín, "I was so young when my story happened to me."

"I was nineteen when most of mine happened," she tells me.

"A few years younger than I was, then. I think." Her words frustrated me, but the lilt of her voice is familiar and soothing. As if I am with a younger Old Song, whose voice does not hurt yet and only offers me comfort.

"I can tell you more of my story," I offer. "If you wish to hear it."

"I do."

Of language and lovers

One morning, when mist shrouded the rocks of Stone Isle and my garment of moss grew cold with moisture, I tugged on my bond with Old Song and flickered to their side.

Song Isle was large—from the sun's rising, there was no seeing the end of land. People of the Song storyline were prosperous. Everyone living wanted a story, to learn how to live, to be soothed, and to hear again and again that there was no need to fear death because when our bodies pass, we don't go any farther than the ancestors' Shoal in the sea. When others visited with people of Song, they brought gifts of fish, moss-woven garments, and colorful rocks to enjoy with the body while it lasts. The Song people were prosperous on their isle, but still Old Song stood alone.

My people say that it is dangerous to wander. That word, danger, in our language, is *tah*. *Re-tah*, toward-danger, means curiosity. *En-tah*, inwards-danger, means yearning. *Ghe-tah*, all-surrounding-danger, means to be alone. All of these words described both Old Song and me.

"I see a red light," I told Old Song. "I close my eyes and drift to sleep, and I hear a song."

"To journey away from the Shoal is dangerous," they said. "You should anchor me here, with your powerful deepnames. Not wander."

"Why do you need to be anchored?" I asked. "And why, of all Stones, must I be the stone to hold you?"

Old Song was unhappy with me. As a Stone, I was not supposed to be curious, just strong; but I was both curious and persistent. It took many tries until Old Song shared their secret with me. Their secret was that they committed a crime.

Old Song had a friend from the Boater storyline, a friend who was bonded to them through their two-syllable deepname. In a perfect world, the Boater storyline would not exist. All bonded people would flicker from one soul to another, traveling without moving between each other without the need for boats. In a perfect world, fish would be plentiful, close to shore. But we fell into this world by necessity, the Star of the Shoal already diminished. Our people are small in numbers and live in an unhospitable sea where the shoals of the fish have been dwindling, and so our way of travel alone is not enough. The Boater people build boats out of pieces of floating wood bound with moss, and these boats carry bodies to fishing grounds, and then carry fish to the isles. These boats also carry floating pieces of wood to make new boats. Sometimes, the boats carry siltway people to isles where they do not have bonds.

Being a Boater is paying too much attention to bodies, and so being in this storyline is dangerous, requiring the constant watchful supervision of Song.

But it was Old Song, in this case, who strayed.

I remember the isles now with different eyes, the eyes of a person trained to notice detail of the world of the body. I remember mist hanging over the stones. The air, full of the beating of gulls' wings. Waves reflecting each other as the sun tumbled lower into the sea. The sound of the fish leaping from the wave. Nothing much changes there, and no change is desired by the Bonded Shoal. But with each year, the fish diminished, requiring the Fish and Boater storylines to stray further and further south.

And there, far to the south, was a coastline. A deep, endless forest of blue-green looming over the waves. Pieces of broken wood came from there, down and out into the sea. In that land, dreamway and nameway people lived together among the towering giants of living wood. These people, too, fished the sea, emptying it even more of sustenance for the living siltway of the Shoal.

Don't venture near those people not ours, instructed the Star of the Shoal through the voices of the Song storyline. *They must not know we exist. That way is danger. Do not yearn for danger.*

But when the curious elder of Song heard this instruction, instead of teaching others not to stray, she herself began to yearn, and so moved us all toward danger.

"She?" Ulín perks up. "You used the language of they for Old Song before."

I tilt my head, impatient. Of all the things, Ulín has latched to this. I grumble. "Yes, *she*, for this language Old Song found for herself in the forest. But first, she asked her Boater bonded to sail south, not to find floating wood or bring back fish, but to witness how your people live."

"I understand her, I think." Ulín chews her lips.

"Of course you do. When you leapt away from your people and toward your serpent prince, you were curious. You wanted to learn his language, you said."

Sunlight is bright in the doorless opening of my room, and it's harder to see Ulín's face now, but I think she blushes. "He taught me more than that."

"Of course he did." I twitch, half-amused, half-frustrated. "Tell me."

Laufkariar did not care about language. He was eager to show her his treasure—a vast coral palace underwater, its rooms inlaid with white pearl and nacre, with emerald and sapphire and bone. It was in that place that Ulín discovered that not all dreamway people could take the serpentshape; most could not, in fact. They only had one shape, like Ulín herself. For the sake of those people, the whole palace domain was sealed with great rooms of air, where one could live a lifetime without taking the serpentshape, and where Ulín did not need to worry about maintaining her magical bubble of breath.

He gifted her with heavy garments sewn with stars made of seed-pearl, and he held Ulín's wrists, binding them with white silver. He said that he would be chosen First Dreamer after his father and she'd be his bride, there on the cushions and under canopies, speechless in his tongue and entirely at his will, while he made agreements and treaties with Ulín's people. Promises of peace. Even though their two peoples had not been at war for centuries.

"It is good that your women inherit," he said.

"I do not want to inherit," she said.

Laufkariar frowned. "Would you let your brother inherit?"

Ulín brushed it off. "My brother is still a child." And why wouldn't he inherit if he wanted? What mattered on the Coast was aptitude and desire and consent, before family name and birth order.

"I want to travel," she told him. "To learn the languages of people not my own, to breathe the air of faraway places, to see and to hear, to study and to be awed, to write down what I learned." When Ulín saw him frown, she quickly added, "But I will always return to you."

Laufkariar's face did not ease—if anything, his frown deepened, but back then, in the dimness, Ulín convinced herself it was a trick of the light. As he held her wrists down, he was tender.

I say to Ulín, "I wish Old Song had found a sea palace when she ventured south." It would have been easier, perhaps, if she befriended people of water.

"What did she find?" Ulín's eyes shine.

Instead of a palace, Old Song found a shore stretching endlessly from side to side, and above it, on a cliff, was a forest. Two peoples lived there—nameway and dreamway—and they came out to greet her, all clothed in garments decorated with twigs and branches. The dreamway shape there was the stag. Old Song described the animal to me, with words she learned later. It was a stag of miracle, its antlers red with dawn and twinkling with jewels like stars underwater. When the stag took a personshape, it was a woman, tall and regal in her nakedness. Three powerful nameway hunters accompanied her, with their bows and their spears of forged steel.

"We will continue to fish the sea," the stag woman said, but her voice was generous. "Our peoples can share its bounty."

She and her husbands welcomed Old Song and her Boater bonded. From the shore they climbed back to the wood, deeper into its dappled green shade. Like deep water, but growing. Old Song described it to me—leaves that rustled like waves, multicolored flowers in glades of foam-soft grass—I have never seen such sights, nor do I understand them still, but I heard Old Song's story and felt her yearning.

The stag woman taught her the words for he, she, and they. And the language of bodies, and their pleasures.

This I learned later: that all boats were forbidden

now, except for the purpose of labor. Not a single person from the Boater storyline would talk to me, and I was steered away from boats on dock.

"Old Song," I said when I flickered to her. "I must know. You traveled and returned without a companion, and now my whole body is buzzing with this yearning. What happened with your Boater bonded? Why do the Boaters turn away from me? When I fall asleep now, I hear a song of red, as if coming from underwater. It beckons and disturbs me."

"Hold me," she asked. "Hold me with your bond. Do not let me go, and do not seek this light which you hear when you drift into sleep. This is not why I bonded with you. You are the anchor, the stone. We must not be traitors to our people."

But I wanted—I knew now, and I wanted. Desire had settled in me, not simply to flicker from one person to another, but—on a surface. On land and on wave. Toward the horizon. To see more than Old Song saw. To see.

Ulín is jotting some words in a notebook spread on her knees. She looks up, and her eyes are shining in a way I do not understand. "There are no words for he, she, and they in siltway?"

"No," I explain, patiently. "The body is not that important."

"It's not just about the body. It's about who the person is, how they feel . . ."

I shrug. "Everybody is equal in the isles. We use the word *en* for all people. I have translated it for you as *they*, but it is not one word out of many. Everyone is *en*." Again, I think, of all my words, this is what she latched on to. But then, didn't Old Song latch onto the word *she* just as fiercely, after that traitorous time she spent with the queen of the stag people? She told me, *"A woman. This I can be—for myself—"*

Ulín smiles at me. "Languages are wonderful, aren't they?"

No, I think. Languages are prisons. People are prisons for each other, too.

"Go on," I say, roughly. "Tell me more of your story."

A woman came to Ulín in secret, at night, when her lover Laufkariar was out hunting. It was his sister. Or perhaps his cousin, or his aunt. A woman just slightly older than him, in her early thirties. She could not take the serpentshape. Like many among his people, she was magicless, and so she would live forever in the underwater palace of nacre and pearl. Her body was lavishly clothed, her dress decorated in shimmering green waves embroidered with slivers of shell, but she did not look happy. She looked afraid.

The woman spoke slowly, making sure Ulín understood her words. And Ulín was hungry for words, so she wrote them down in her notebook, to study later. But now she raised her head from the page and gave words to this dreamway woman, who was some twelve years her senior. Ulín was just newly nineteen.

"Is it true that in your land, your women inherit? He told me so," the woman said.

"This is not how we live," Ulín said. "I could inherit if I wanted to, and if my people approved of me. But I have no desire to govern, so it will not even come to a vote."

"But your brother," the dreamway woman said. "He is a man."

Ulín shrugged. "He might or might not be. He is a child. Thirteen. At his first gathering, my sibling might adopt the language of she or he, or declare themself ichidi and adopt the language of they. It is too early to know."

Ulín did not mean to say anything inappropriate or weird. She learned only later that among the serpent people, statements like these were admissions of shame. Admissions of deviance. Invitations to hate.

I say, "You were simply sharing your language. You thought your sibling could have been an ichidi . . ." The word is a familiar weight in my mouth, a yearning for someone who taught me the word, someone who is no longer here.

Ulín smiles at me. "You pronounced it perfectly."

I look away from her, stilling my features. "In the tongues of the desert, such people are called in-between-ers. In the siltway tongue, there are no words like that. Nor words for *woman* or *man*. Nobody is different from another person."

"Perhaps you are all in-betweeners," Ulín speaks as if it's a jest. But it's not.

"No," I say. "It's not that. It's that a single person is unimportant. We are a collective. The language of I itself is discouraged, even though many use it."

"I would love to hear more," she tells me, warm.

"I will tell you more. But not yet. First, I want more of your story."

Laufkariar came in the night. He had hunted in serpentshape in the dreaming sea that stretches above the waking lands. Only the strongest of dreamway hunters could ascend there, and for him it was easy, to leap up in serpentshape, leaving nothing behind. Ulín had always admired him for it. His power. His prowess. Now his breath smelled of lilac, and in his violet eyes were reflected his kills—dreaming fish and porpoises; aquatic birds; even serpents. Ulín did not think it violent—these were only dreams, after all. He hovered above her, his smile of hunger and need, and he was the handsomest of men, and she wanted—

She wanted to show him her notebook.

"Look, I am learning your language," she said. "I'm making such interesting discoveries. For example—"

Laufkariar looked frustrated at first, uninterested. Then he grabbed the pages.

"Who said all this?"

"Oh, your sister, I think." Ulín described her to him. "She's helping me learn."

"You are naïve, nameway woman," he said. Then: "Beloved."

His gaze was dark, but he bent to kiss her, and Ulín's breath caught. Her whole body yearned for him, just like her mind yearned for words and their meaning.

"She is simply jealous," he said. "Jealous that she can never inherit. Jealous and weak. She's not even a hunter. Don't worry."

Ulín was falling asleep when he stepped out of the room.

Ulín breathes deep. Looks away. "Can you teach me a word? Any word?"

She needs a break, I guess. And I don't mind.

"All right." What shall I teach her, then? "*Rordan* is a word that means inwards-toward-the-center-of-dan. Roh-ereh-dan. *Dan* is the thing which is stable."

"Stable like a stone?" Ulín leafs through the notebook. "Like kah and kahir?"

"No, not like a stone. *Dan* means the solidity and center of people. *Rordan* is the centered, stable thing which is all of us. A collective. Perhaps you would say in your language, a *family*."

"I'd say . . . a *house*," she offers.

I do not understand. "A dwelling?"

She nods. "A dwelling which is a center of people. For me, it's the house of my ancestor Ranra. Once, in our Coastal language, the word *house* meant *ship*."

She explains the word for me—a ship is a kind of

47

boat, but larger and steadier than the one my people would make out of driftwood. Now *House* Ranravan is a dwelling, and a name for Ranra's people—her descendants, and their lovers, and their friends, and their children.

I know this name.

It is a lurching, dizzying feeling; a coincidence, maybe. I could ask, but I'm wary of where the story will lead us—lead me. After a moment I school my features and continue my tale.

Rordan is a word that means the whole of the Bonded Shoal. The star made of ancestors, shallowly connected to the world of the living and nurtured by it. But the past is reachable, if one so desires. If one wants to talk to the ancestors, one has to descend centerward, travel down the bonds.

Among the living, this is rarely done. What reason is there to go so deep into the Shoal? The task of the living is to live. To work, to maintain the body, to share it so that more siltway bodies can be born. The living are simply an anchor for the Star of the Shoal, a safeguard so that it won't diminish again. What purpose, what curiosity, would move a single one of us to descend into the Shoal of the dead?

Yet it is known to happen. The one who birthed me taught me to do this before they abandoned the body, if I needed to find them again. And so at night I lay down in the shallow pool in my cave, and tugged on the ancestor-bond through my two-syllable deepname.

It was quiet and silvery-gray in the ancestor Shoal, and my parent did not stir when I flickered to their side. They had a personshape in the water of that place, with eyes of pale silver that stared past me, and a mouth that spoke nothing. I wanted to talk to them, or simply be by their side, but I was afraid to linger.

My parent's soul was bonded to others, I saw—people of their own generation, and the preceding one. I tugged on that vertical bond, and descended through the bonds of the dead.

There were so many bonds. I did not understand this geometry. More than one bond could be formed through a deepname. Old Song told me about it, but nobody taught me how. Yet I could not stay to figure it out. If I thought too much, I would find myself back in the pool in my cave, my residual gills stretched taut with the labor of breath.

No, I had to keep moving, and so I pulled myself down centerward, generation after generation. These people were unfamiliar to me. Their bonds were strange, and they looked translucent, leached of color, with little awareness of me—but the more I descended, the more I sensed that I was being watched, as if all of them watched me at once.

It was foreboding and dreary and I could not imagine moving to live here. This was what death was about, what we all wanted at the end of a life—to be free from the body and its labor, to continue in the ancestor Shoal. Why did it feel so constricting? I was frightened, and wanted to flicker back out and up to the living, all the way to Old Song. I hovered, motionless, by one of my great-great-ancestors, seventy generations deep.

Just then, a song began to ascend from deeper inwards below. A song I thought I recognized.

I am Stone, I told myself. *I am strong.* Strong enough to anchor the isles. Strong enough to anchor Old Song. *I am Stone. I am a warrior.*

So I moved deeper down, and in a few generations I began to see the red light.

The color was coming from inside a cluster of ancestors, all bonded together. Each of these ancestors had a translucent body, whitish, but formed around a red light that colored the edges of their arms in a pink glow. These ancestors moved around in the water, all looking at me.

> *We are Song and Stone*, they sang, *from before*
> *the Star of the Shoal came to this world*
> *and sank into this sea. We are the youngest of*
> *travelers, the last unalive generation.*
> *We are the ones who saw and heard when the*
> *twelve stars were carried upon Bird's burning tail.*
> *We saw HIM and heard HIM calling to us and*
> *We wanted to fall—*
> *Into the embrace of Ladder's hands.*
> *But we were overruled.*

I did not know back then who Ladder was, but the language was familiar from Old Song's story. *He*: a *man* from elsewhere. A nameway.

I want to travel, I said. *Not only to flicker, but in the body. I want to know this world of the other eleven stars that fell and were embraced by their keepers.*

There was a disturbance in the Shoal.

If you want to know about Ladder, an ancestor sang,
then you must attend to his summoning song.
We heard it. We hear it still.
If you attend to it, he will call you, like he called
us—and you will travel to him.

The whole of the Shoal began to swirl. Above and below, souls streaked past me, fishlike, agitated, dissolving
their bonds and darting away. I'd never thought such a
thing possible, but I felt it as deep pain, agitation. Fear.
In a moment, it was as if the whole Shoal had separated
into its constituent souls. They were silver sea-minnows
rushing this way and that, dizzying me. In that moment,
I perceived a cluster of people still clumped in the water,
unmoving. These were the red-glowing ancestors.

They did not seem fishlike. Neither did they separate.

They were bonded—not just to each other—I
squinted, to see—they were held by the bonds that
extended toward them. Not lovingly, or even compan-
ionably were they held—no, this was made to constrain
them, and—I perceived this—to punish.

Just as the Shoal separated, these bonds too began
to weaken, to wink in and out, and the ancestors of red
began to struggle, throwing themselves against the con-
straint of these flaring and fizzling bonds that held
them in place.

All this took only a moment, a frantic and terrible
moment.

The Shoal flared, blinding me as it reformed.

The Shoal.

The Shoal was still.

All was as silent and unmoving as before.

No, more than before—the ancestors of red neither sang nor spoke. They still had bodies of people, motionless now, their eyes flat and staring past me.

I wanted to call out to them, but could not find my voice. And something within the Shoal was still focused on me. The whole Star of the Shoal, its consciousness.

I tried to swim up and away from this attention, but now all the bonded but unconstrained souls in the Shoal were turning toward me, from above, from below, from the sides—pressing in. Suffocating—I did not know if I even breathed. A feeling of dread seized me, and I knew that if I stayed, I would be counted, accounted for, I would be judged by the collective which was the Star of the Shoal. I, too, would be bound and constrained with those who now hovered motionless, glowing a dull red—those deemed too dangerous to the collective.

In my fear, I tugged with all my might upon my living bond. The bond with Old Song. In a moment, I flickered out and upward, toward her. To Song Isle.

It was raining, sweet drizzles upon the clammy skin of my face. Breath came in and out of my nostrils, filled my lungs with beautiful, cool surface-air. I opened my mouth, devouring the raindrops. I lay there, spread on the stones. Just breathing. Alive. Alive.

Somewhere above me, Old Song was yelling. I did not understand. Then I felt pain. She was kicking me with her feet. Away from her, into the water by Song Isle. I did not understand her words.

I do not remember how I got back to Stone Isle. Did I get there at all? There was a cave, perhaps my own. A shallow pool. My whole body felt as if aflame. I was delirious. I sank down into the water of the pool, opening and closing my gills. In my ears, Old Song's yelling now coalesced into words. She said she loved me, but I betrayed her—endangered her. That she had transgressed enough. That she needed me to hold her.

I covered my ears with my hands and sank deeper. Behind my closed eyelids I saw the connections of light, remembering how the Shoal had separated for a brief, sharp moment.

Then it reformed. Around the prison.

I shudder with the vividness of memory. My gills open and close and I cough, half-suffocating in the dry, too-warm air of my room. Ulín makes a motion toward me, but I wave her off. I rise, dip my hands in the tepid water of my pool and rub my sides up to the gills, easing the pain just slightly. The water would need changing soon.

I expect Ulín to ogle, but she is looking aside, giving me privacy. The feeling of her kindness is strange, like a pinch on my arm. I did not expect it. I don't know if I like it.

"She told you she loved you," Ulín says at last.

I swallow, my mouth painfully dry, my gills barely better. "She said so, but I don't know if she ever did."

"Her fear outweighed her love." Ulín's face is still, as if she is holding back even more words. Perhaps she shouldn't.

"Can you take over for a bit?" I ask her.

In the palace of nacre

Ulín did not see the sister again, but Laufkariar was wonderful. So attentive and tender. He even helped her learn the language of the serpents. He asked his people to help Ulín, and they would come to speak with her. Mostly these were women—noblewomen and servants. She learned the language from them. They were friendly, and Ulín wrote down many words.

She missed the library at Ranra's Towers, and she wondered if the university would have an even larger library. But Laufkariar did not think she should go anywhere. The university in particular was a nameway place, he said, and Ulín was to live among the dreamway, by his side. He wanted them to be married.

When Ulín agreed to get married, she thought how much she wanted to be a part of his people's ceremony. It would have splendid foods and poetry, musical instruments and underwater games. The serpent people's weddings seemed much more elaborate and magical than what happened on the Coast, where people rarely married a single person. Her parents had that kind of union, but it was more common to simply live in *houses*, with many lovers and their lovers and their friends. Ulín knew that she did not want many lovers. It was more than enough to have one.

If Ulín hesitated about the marriage, she tried not to dwell on it. She loved his language, and she loved his people and she loved him. Laufkariar was splendid, magnificent. And he wanted her. And he was so *interesting*; even his moods, perhaps especially his moods. She was only nineteen.

He gave her so many gifts—clothes and jewelry unrivaled. He gave her a chest of treasure from ancient treaties—gifts given to his people by Ranra herself when she was crossing the sea. Then there was the pen—a splendid mechanical pen with a hidden ink chamber and a long, graceful nib. It had a body like a feather made of tiny diamonds. The heart of the feather was a ruby that glittered every time Ulín moved to write something down, distracting her with its fractured light.

He'd leave, sometimes in the night, to hunt in the dreaming sea, accompanied by his three companions. Ulín did not give this much thought. He would return in good spirits, smelling of lilacs and death. And he smiled, as if he knew things she did not, and that was exciting. Ulín would ask him to tell her about the dreaming sea, and she wrote down the words he used to describe the dreamhunt. She was happy, she thought, alight with curiosity and always learning more.

He did not want Ulín's brother to be at the wedding.

She was not a friend of her sibling. He was entering adolescence, and he was strange those days, full of anger and angles. It was difficult to talk to him. Ulín rarely tried. But he was her brother, after all.

"He is askew," Laufkariar said harshly. "Neither a man nor a woman." Later, Ulín remembered that she told that to his sister.

"It is too early to know," she replied, defensive but not comprehending his vehemence. "My brother uses the language of he, and has not yet attended his first gathering."

"He likes men," Laufkariar snarled. "This is a perversion."

Later, Ulín thought she should have asked him how he knew her brother's preference. Back then she said, "All my people are like this."

Perhaps Laufkariar did not understand. She had to make him understand. "Our customs are different from yours. We are free in our loves and multiple in our preferences—"

He interrupted. "No. You love me."

That, too, is a preference, she thought. Aloud she said, "I only and always love you."

Laufkariar's eyes glinted in the dark of the nighttime chamber. "Your little brother is jealous. He spies on the two of us when we visit your land. Perhaps he wants to inherit. Perhaps he wants me." His lips twisted in anger.

"He's a child."

"No. You despise him. And fear him, perhaps?" he asked.

Ulín wanted to deny that word, *despise*, but for some reason she did not. "Why should I fear him? He only has a single deepname. He is strange, but he never did anything bad that I know of." It was an odd thing to say, as if she thought he did bad things that she did not know of, this sibling who was no longer a child, with his burning gaze and a single two-syllable deepname, a child-not-child who wanted to hover when Ulín was around, and that was not what she wanted. She was an adult now, soon to be married. She wanted to be with other adults.

Ulín felt odd, defensive. "I don't talk to him much because he is young and has no interest in language."

Laufkariar kissed her on the lips, as if she'd said too much, and perhaps she had. For long hours, all was forgotten.

I stare at Ulín, holding myself back from speaking. Her sibling scared her—but he did not do anything. Was that enough to despise a child?

I say, "In the Shoal, one must not ever be different from others. Not even *feel* different. That is something to correct."

Ulín goes still under my gaze. "I understand."

"Is difference punished on your Coast?"

"No, we . . ." She gulps and shudders. "No, we welcome all."

"I see." I do not see. Not clearly, and not yet. All I know is that greatest despair finds its way to this court. I am here, and so is she.

"Were you—" Ulín says, "were you corrected, when you returned from the Shoal of the dead?"

"Of course I was."

The judgment of many

When I awoke in the cave—I am still not sure if it was mine—there were other people with me. People of the Song storyline, and a few familiar Stones, and some people of Moss whom I did not know. Nobody ever comes to a sleeping cave if they do not want to share bodies. But these people pressed around, suffocating me in the body, like that feeling I had when I was deep in the Shoal. I tried to edge away, but there was no room; I was still in the pool, and other people were everywhere. Even in the pool.

Someone of the Moss storyline bent over me. In their hands was a braid of moss, a strong, thin woven rope, and they bound my wrists. I struggled instinctively, shocked. Remembering how the ancestors of red were bound. I tried to speak, to ask, but breath deserted me. My gills opened and closed, but I was out of water, and my land-breath refused to switch over.

"Don't struggle," an elder of Stone said.

Ulín gasps. "Struggle—did they use a verb?"

I snap, "No, of course they did not use a verb. They said, *Not-from-you-at-us-force-away*." What in Bird's name is *wrong* with her, to interrupt at this moment to ask about a word?

Ulín whispers, "Sorry . . ."

"I am translating, always." But when I think of it now, I remember the Stone elder's lips move, and in my mind, the nameway words *Don't struggle* echo in my mind. An angry, dizzying feeling floods me. I do not want to think about who I have become, how even my thoughts are in nameway now. "Do you even want me to continue?" I ask her.

"Yes, please, I am sorry . . ."

I shush her. "Then listen."

"Don't struggle." The Stone elder's voice was soothing. "Come out to the water and wind. No decisions have yet been made, but you must stand judgment, surrounded by the collective."

They were already moving me by these bonds, pulling me out of the pool, to the stone ground of the cave among them, then outside, to the water and wind. Mist hung in the air. It was hard to know what isle this was. I could barely see in the fog—shapes, familiar and new, dense all around me. I sensed Old Song nearby, standing in stiffness, and I wondered if she, too, was bound.

The elder of Stone spoke. "We are all around ourselves here, living elders of the Shoal, and through us the ancestors, gathered for this difficulty."

Then came a deep, resonant voice I did not recognize. "We are for the judgment of these two judged ones, bonded ones. My people of the Moss storyline, here for both the judged persons of Stone and Song. People of the Song storyline, here only for the judged person of Stone. People of Stone storyline, here for the judged person of Song. Thus we are gathered in justice, no one judging one's own storyline." This was the elder called Moss-deep, I learned later.

The third voice was ancient and lilting, more ancient by far than Old Song. I had met them before, briefly, when I visited Song Isle. This elder was called Song-mist. "The deep Shoal is disturbed," they sang. "So gather round, and let us begin the judgment of the living rordan."

The Stone people stepped closer, and I could make out their features through the mist, but I looked away. The Stone elder spoke now, toward Old Song.

"When you and the severed one from the Boater storyline strayed from the isles, we still kept you among us. We let you live and gave you an elder's name, because you are weighty and wise, and the voice of your song was allowed to continue among us, as one of us. *On one condition.*"

"I did not stray away from the rordan," wailed Old Song, and her voice was piercing, unsettling. "I bonded with this Stone to hold me, but this Stone strayed, and their weight—"

Elder Song-mist now spoke to me. "You went down centerward into the Shoal, disturbing the ancestors, and ourselves. Who incited you toward this disturbance? Was it your new Song bonded?"

"Did Old Song make you stray? You lived quietly before," said Elder Moss-deep.

I did not much remember what came before Old Song. Days on end, days of labor, much of it helping the people of the Fish and Moss storylines; days wondering why I was a Stone, and what was the task of the Stones; nights floating in my pool, and trying to see with my eyes all the stars below and above the dividing line of the wave. I did not much share my body, and I did not produce any new bodies of my own. There was not much story before Old Song and her stories.

"I did not do anything to make this Stone stray," screamed Old Song, and I wondered if she was ill. Why was her voice this loud, this desperate? "I bonded with them to anchor me, like you told me. I did nothing else."

"Did you tell them about your crime?" said Moss-deep. There was a movement, and Old Song screamed again, a long, shrill, terrifying sound that did not make sense. Then the elder Moss-deep turned to me. "What stories did Old Song tell you to push you to do this, you who worked hard for the living collective and had stayed quiet before?"

All of the judging ones waited for me to betray Old Song, to say that her stories led me astray from the isles. I could feel it, palpable, in the air. They wanted me to cast Old Song away, just like she had cast me away when they pressed her.

But I did not want to.

I looked closer at that feeling of mine, stubborn and

centered in me like a smooth gray pebble. I remembered how Old Song came to me for the first time. She said *You are strong, a match to my pain*, and this was, after all, the forgotten purpose of Stones.

Soon I found out why Old Song screamed, because they began to push and jostle me in the same way, to prod me with jagged rocks and with their hands. I could not defend myself; I was bound, but by now I knew I was strong. I wanted to be even stronger. I wanted to be like the stones in the sea, no matter what happens. Resolute. Silent.

I take a breath, but it is not enough. I tell Ulín, "I need a moment. Do you want to take over?"

She is silent and swaying, rocking back and forth. Not looking at me.

Understanding unfolds in me, slow. "My story reminded you of something painful."

"It's all right," she says, but it isn't. She is pale. "I can . . ."

"You do not want to remember."

She mumbles, "I owe you . . ."

I speak fast, unthinking. "No. No! You owe me nothing. Please, I will not force you." I have no idea why I feel protective of a stranger who has been sitting here all this time without saying the name of her target. But she—she listened to me, as if she wanted to know my story, and I wonder if anybody else had before.

Not Old Song, or even Ladder.

Only a single person before.

I rub my forehead and get up. Offer Ulín an earthenware cup of drinking water. "Here, take this—or would you rather have tea?"

She nods, still not looking at me. "Can we share? If it's not too much bother . . ."

I nod with her. "We can. I have tea leaves from Lepaleh."

"Please," she says. I exhale. We can drink tea together. There is no rush.

Later, the tea cups comforting in our palms, she asks me what will happen if she won't be able to trade stories with me anymore.

I shrug. "We could sit here together, until we figure this out." There is a feeling of calm in me now, a warm feeling like the moss that blooms on the siltway isles in early autumn. It's been years since I felt this.

I tell her, "I can continue now, if you wish. Do not worry about your story."

Ulín tries to thank me, but there is no need. I understand.

After the judgment, they put me in another cave. This one certainly wasn't mine. It was larger, and echoing, and in the walls I saw hooks which were chiseled from stone. Fragments of ancient moss rope hung from some of them, but I was the only one in the cave. Perhaps at some earlier time, others had been held here.

My judgment could not be given before the judgment of Old Song. I have learned that I was unimportant, but perhaps just a bit more important than the Boater person they severed and cast out of the Shoal. But Old Song was a part of everything.

Before, I did not think that one person could be more important than others, in the Shoal. We were supposed to be equal, and equally held in the Shoal, held by each other and for each other. Perhaps the word *important* is not the word which is needed. Nevertheless, I was in the cave and waiting, while Old Song was receiving judgment.

I lay very still. Very still. The echo of Moss-deep's voice reverberated through stone and into the cavern.

"There is danger to the Shoal in straying, in deviance. This happened before—you, Old Song, of all people, should know this. We must stay together, otherwise we are not the Shoal. We cannot trust people not our own. They might tell stories of welcome, but then they will take our water, and take all our fish, even though they have woods that are teeming with food, and they'll trick us one by one to stray from the collective, and then, before long, the whole world will be dying.

"You of all people, should know this.

"And if you did not do anything, and it was all Stone, then you know what to do.

"Tell us. Tell us if it was all Stone's doing. Stone's crime."

Eventually, she did. She blamed me for everything.

Late at night, Old Song came. I did not know that at first; I was sleeping. My hands were still bound, and I could not find comfort. My gills opened and closed laboriously in the shallow, cold pool. She grasped me by the leg, and I came to the surface, shaking and sputtering.

I am so sorry, she said. Then she tore at our bond, and suddenly my head was splitting, and it felt like she was tearing out my whole mind, my tongue—

When I speak of this, Ulín cries out, and her hands grasp her cheeks, the sides of her head, bruising-tight. Her eyes are wild, frightened.

Oh. My story. Her nameloss—my words must have reminded her.

She rocks and says again and again, "I'm sorry. I'm sorry."

I stretch out my hand, an offer, and she reaches to me as if drowning. Her fingers clench tight. "I'm sorry . . . I'm sorry . . ."

"Please," I say. "No need to apologize. I can stop if you need me to."

"Did you lose your magic?" she whispers.

"No, I kept both my deepnames. But the bond was gone."

We clasp each other's hands in the semidarkness of my room and breathe together until she is ready to listen again.

I'd gone without a living bond before, hoping for a companion who would also share their body with me, but then I met Old Song, and I did not want anyone else.

I wanted—I wanted to keep that feeling of her, that warmth, curiosity, wonder, her stories most of all. She told me she loved me, and I felt it—but now she had severed our bond.

Then she touched me, and I recoiled, but she only unbound my hands.

"You did not speak against me in judgment," she whispered, "even though I betrayed you. Even now, I betrayed you again. I'm so sorry. I am not brave or strong like you are, and I cannot abide to be severed. The collective will find me someone else to bond to, someone of their choosing. But I convinced them that there is hope for you, that you can be corrected. The collective will give you another chance. If you speak to them humbly, for you they too will find a new bond. It will be as it should be."

"Nothing is as it should be." I grasped her arm, and she all but recoiled, but I held her. I was strong.

Later, I wondered why she did not simply flicker away from me. Back then, in my exhaustion and hurt, I leaned into the power of my insignificant body. The stone strength of it.

Old Song had kicked me before, and hurt me, and shielded herself from judgment with a story which hid many truths. She had severed our bond, and hurt me so much; my head was reeling, and under my tongue was the bitterness of vomit. I thought I could strike back now. I could hurt her in the body, even kill her. What did I have to lose? I did not want to be *corrected*. To be bonded with a prison-bond, to live a dutiful quiet life, to die into the Shoal and be there motionless and bound forever, without even Old Song to speak to. Or to be severed, and die without a Shoal to take my soul, to perish without a trace like those who were torn away into the void. There were no good ways forward. All was despair.

Within me, the deep music of red surged and faded.

Old Song did not struggle. Did not flicker away.

I held her, and my eyes adjusted. She had already been hurt in the body, like I had been hurt, but I paid little attention to my wounds. She was cut and punched, and she was bleeding, but above all, I saw that she was deeply afraid. Afraid of the hurt in the body. Afraid of the people who hurt her. Afraid of being alone.

"Tell me a story," I said. "One last time, Old Song."

She shuddered and whimpered, but I held her, and she stayed.

"Tell me a story of something that matters to you. You owe me that much."

She whispered, "The stag woman. She was the Kran-Valadar, the queen of the dreamway and name-way hunters I met in the south. She called me beautiful and beloved, and she held me. She called me the wise-woman of the fish people and the singer of their tales, and she taught me the word for woman in the tongue of her people."

"Kälu." Ulín's eyes shine with something like joy as she speaks the word Old Song has given me back then. Woman.

I am shocked to hear it from Ulín's mouth. "Have you studied the language of the stag people?" I say.

She looks oddly embarrassed, and pleased. "Not as such. A little bit." She tells me how, in a strange little shop in the middle of nowhere, she bought a dictionary. She studied the stag people's tongue to compare it to the tongue of the serpents. "I found many similar words in these languages," Ulín says, her voice warm with pride. "In the tongue of the serpents, woman is *kaloy*."

"How many languages did you learn?" Even two had been hard for me.

"There is always so much more to learn," she says, evasive. Her eyes are bright, and I'm glad she is feeling better.

"*Woman*," I say. "In my language, we do not have words like these. Perhaps we had them once, before the Shoal journeyed through the void. But we don't anymore. There is a person who carries and births from their body, and there are those who do not. This is merely a difference of labor." I did not birth anyone, so it was not my labor. But back in the prison-cave, Old Song had whispered to me, "I am a coward, Stone. But one day I could be brave. I could choose. To be who I want to be. To be a *woman*. And you . . . you could be a *woman* too."

This thing she had to give. A blessing, a curse, a despair, a rebellion.

For years, I have cherished it.

Ulín breathes deep, her eyes on mine. "I think I am ready to tell you more, now." Ulín speaks so prettily, I think, even in a language not her own. I struggle with it sometimes.

"Don't rush," I say. "You can tell me as much as you can."

The severing

Ulín went home for a while, to prepare for the wedding. Laufkariar escorted her out of the sea palace. Ulín's father had sent emissaries. He was suspicious and angry—did the prince of the serpents imprison his daughter under the wave? She told him it was all right.

In a large room overlooking the sea, Ulín met with her parents to make wedding plans. It was chilly, and the windows were open. She inhaled the smell of sea and pines, her skin drinking in the autumn light. How marvelous, to have a room with windows, a room full of air that came in and out. To listen to birdsong. Certainly Laufkariar would allow his bride the pleasure of spending time here, with her family. Perhaps she could still go to the university. She would always return, after all.

Doubt, a small bird, nestled in her ribcage. It was inobtrusive and hidden, and yet it rustled there, turning its delicate beak this way and that. But before Ulín could even name this bird, her father's anger expanded, choking out air.

"This marriage is wrong," he said. "I do not trust the serpent people—in peace now, but our ancient enemies— yes, there's peace now and been for a while, but what reason other than politics is there for such a marriage?"

"I don't know," said Ulín's parent.

"Your mother, or your father?" I ask, to be sure.

"My other parent, Sibeli. They are ichidi. My father is Kannar."

I nod.

"I don't know," Sibeli said. "They could be in love. Laufkariar could love her."

Ulín's father replied, "He is seven years her senior. Twenty-six, and they marry young, and he could not find a bride among his people? This is a pile of guano."

I'm right here, Ulín wanted to say. *Stop discussing me as if I'm nothing.* But when she spoke, she tried to sound reasonable, adultlike. "The age difference is not a problem for me—you yourself have lovers both older and younger, and so does most everyone on the Coast."

"He's aiming for First Dreamer." Her father spoke loud and fast. "This is a power play, he wants to rule, and my daughter will be a means to this end. You don't see it because you are still a child, I will not allow this to go forward."

If Ulín were to say, *I am not a child,* it would come

out childish. She steeled herself. "I only want peace between our peoples."

He said, "There already was peace between our peoples before this whole thing began!"

She wanted to stopper her ears and scream, but Kannar's anger upset her beyond her ability to express. His three-deepname configuration of three single-syllable deepnames, the Warlord's Triangle, made her father both irritable and incredibly powerful, but he had never before turned to Ulín in anger. She had been, until this moment, the smart and learned child, the beloved and beautiful child, the responsible, brilliant child with a future in governance once Kannar himself retired. She had not told him yet that she had no interest in governance.

Never before did his anger turn toward her, and now it felt like everything was falling apart. Did her father not love her? Did her father not want her to make her own choices?

"Do you love Laufkariar?" Sibeli asked Ulín.

"Yes," she yelled, even though her parent did not yell. Ulín was louder even than her father. The small bird of doubt was shocked into silence. "I love him, I want to be with him, I am no different from anyone else on the Coast who is free to take lovers!"

"You want to be *married*, Ulín, according to the customs of *his people*," her father said. "Even here, such a ceremony holds a heavy weight, and is rarely undertaken. Among the serpent people, even among other nameway people who do not share our Coastal ways, a marriage means so much, a marriage can mean forever, and you cannot expect me to support—"

The bird of doubt stirred again at his words, but then Sibeli said, "She is of age."

"Newly of age," Kannar roared. "As soon as she was of age, he was on the prowl—"

Sibeli continued, as calm as if those words weren't spoken. "Ulín is not lesser than him, than anyone. She must have freedom to make her own decisions. If it is a mistake, then she will make it of her own free will. If later she walks away of her own free will, then we will be here."

"I will not abide—my child gone from me for years— to live underwater, of all places—"

Pain shot through Ulín's head and her ears filled with noise. She ran out of the chamber, down the familiar, age-worn stone stairs. It felt good to be home, good to run, but more than anything else she wanted to be away from her parents, away from everyone, under the open sky. There, on the small secluded beach between jagged rocks, she paced among the stones, trying not to look out to the sea. Ulín did not want her lover or her father to find her—she needed time to think—but it was her brother who found her.

I touch Ulín's hand again as she gulps for air. "Do you want to stop? A sip of tea?"

She shakes her head. "I must press on before I lose my courage."

"Forgive me," I say. "I understand." I take another breath, and another, then tell her that I am ready to hear.

Tajer had just turned fourteen a few weeks ago. He was awkward and moody, and when she returned from the wave, the two of them barely exchanged greetings. There was something odd about her sibling, something strange and powerful and different, like a graceful but venomous snake, even though Ulín did not want to think of her own brother that way.

There was nothing graceful about him when he found her on the beach. He was bloodied, disheveled, in torn clothes, with bloodshot and bulging eyes. And his presence was powerful, off-kilter, suffocating, as if there was no more air.

Before she could think about it, or ask him anything, he yelled, "What in Bird's name did you tell him about me?"

Guilt and defiance churned in her gut. "You always spied on me—on us—"

He laughed, a startling, ugly sound, more a scream than a laugh. "Did you tell him I'm jealous? Less than a man?"

I told him you could be ichidi. I did not mean anything by it. The serpents—they think differently about things—

She could have said that. Apologized. But she didn't. Anger at her family churned in her, and guilt, and a fierce defiance. None of them honored her. All of them hated her choice; they all hated Laufkariar. Ulín yelled, "You *were* jealous—he is my betrothed—"

"You're always the favorite—better than everyone—

at least do not marry the Bird-plucked bastard, Ulín . . ." His voice shook. "At least that—or did you *plan* this? You *planned* this?"

Tajer swung his arms as he screamed, and Ulín could have retreated, but instead she pulled on her deep-names. One-syllable and two-syllables. She used to be so much stronger—

I shudder, and my fingers dig into my palms. The famil-iar name, the terrible spiraling of the story as it rushes inward toward darkness, ready to devour itself.

"Are you—" Ulín asks.

I do not want to hear. It is too much.

I promised to witness.

No, I want to. I want to witness.

I exhale. "I am ready. Go on."

Ulín was used to being so much magically stronger than her brother—he'd only had the two-syllable deepname. But something felt different now, because her brother—the one with the two-syllable deepname, the one who had been so much weaker, so much more of a child—he had *more*. His deepnames—more than one, more than two, more more more—

She could not stop now. She yelled, "Don't deny it, you wanted him—"

His deepnames formed blinding, rotating structures

over her head, like a whirlwind that shook with lightning. Both of them yelled, their words swallowed by that whirlwind. The weight of his magical structure descended upon her, and all was dark.

When Ulín awoke, her father was by her side.

A splitting headache.

Later, she was told that her deepnames were burned out. It was her brother who called for help, and then helped carry her in. He was in his rooms now, under guard.

So . . . finally, the target is revealed. My mouth feels bitter. "How long ago was this?" I ask.

"Ten years."

Her story left me raw, and my words come harsher than I want them to. "What makes you want to seek your brother's death now?" I thought it would be her serpent prince. Laufkariar. That would make sense. The serpent people live underwater, and I can move underwater. But this—

I grimace at my own insight. "The Headmaster sent you to me."

She looks confused. "Why are you angry?"

"Forgive me," I mutter. "I am not angry, I'm just—"

I wish the Headmaster asked me first. But he knew I would take any contract if I wanted to graduate and get out of here.

Ulín tries to get up, her eyes dry and empty as if she's newly injured. "Forgive me. I will ask for someone else."

"No!" I speak before thinking. "I do not want you to leave."

I take a deep breath. It is moments like this which hold an answer to everything. Anger clears the mind and makes you stronger, as long as you trust your own judgment. Somebody came here and taught me that. I say, "The target is your choice."

Ulín sits down again, shakes her head ruefully. "I'll be honest, I am still not sure about the target. It could be my brother, or someone else."

I say, "There's more to your story. And mine."

"Yes." She wraps her hands around her empty teacup. "Do you want maybe . . . to tell me more?"

Yes, I do.

After Old Song left the prison-cave, I lay in the pool, tasting salt water and blood. The severed bond burned like a lashing of storm against skin. But even more than the pain, my anger burned red-hot. I had never before felt anything like it. It was exhilarating and terrifying, that despair—yes, despair. The isles themselves, my people, my whole life, were ash and blood on my tongue. Old Song still had living bonds and could flicker away, but I was motionless. Before I bonded with Old Song, this did not bother me—I lived simply on Stone Isle, like others, and if I wanted to leave Stone Isle, I could form a temporary bond with someone, or ask a Boater person for passage. I do not much remember those days before Old Song, now. Gray on gray, and the water lapping. Was I happy? Was there even a word? I do not recall.

I was a prisoner now, and the only way out of here lay through the gathered will of others. Perhaps in time I would bond again. I would be told that I belonged, again. I would birth new bodies and raise them to bond, to live quietly in the collective. And when I died, I would be held in the Shoal underwater, like the ancestors of red.

This had been my life before and I was content with it, but now all I felt was despair. I would not live like this. I, whose Stone storyline had lost its meaning—but not its place in our long passage through the void—I was weightier than my imprisonment.

I sank deeper into the cold water, and tugged on my remaining bond. My parent, the one who birthed me, hovering fearfully on the edges of the Shoal of the dead. I sensed that my parent wanted to talk to me, chide me, but I had no time. I pushed away from them, deeper into the Shoal.

It was only a matter of time before I would be noticed.

Years later, it occurred to me that I could have stolen a Boater's boat and rowed all the way to the shore of Lysinar, but I did not think this way. This is a nameway thing to think. I learned how to think this way from the nameway people, and I cannot unlearn it now, so I can never be translated back to my own people. I fear that in time I will forget my language. Maybe even my shape. I cannot become a nameway or a dreamway person, but I'm not like I had been. Some different, new thing.

Where was I? Traveling deeper centerward into the ancestral Shoal.

At last, I reached the ancestors of red. They looked even more distorted behind the glowing bars of their bonds, as if they had screamed themselves raw—but now they were silent. Around me the Shoal was swirling. The intelligence I perceived in it was not any single ancestor, but a togetherness. The soul-minnows moved and separated and moved again, pressing me in, crowding around me. I was too small to notice, that first time I came here, but now the Shoal knew me and thought me dangerous. I was not supposed to come back, not until death, and even then my place would be on the shallow outskirts of the collective. This deep place wasn't my place.

The Shoal's pressure became pain, even though I was not here in the body, only as my spirit, but the pain was pressure in my spectral ears, in my spectral throat. Somewhere on the surface, my body thrashed in the pool.

Thoughts rushed through me, like song. That red song. If it could be heard here, in this ancient and hostile deep, then I could follow it like a bond. But I wanted, I wanted to know, to make sense of it all—the Shoal, these ancestors of Stone, the red color, my people, my story. So I shouted—it came out a hoarse, ragged whisper—

"Why? Why do you imprison them?"

The voice of the Star of the Shoal was thunder that rocked me and choked me, grander and grander, blooming around me, swallowing me.

You want a story? Listen. Listen before you are no more.

Long time ago, the Shoal was not unified. Freedom, cried some. This word you do not know. It has been erased from our language. Freedom! To-be-whole-in-one's-will, without-others—this freedom was deemed more important than the collective. So the original Shoal had let many people break away—even though we protested, we were overruled. Freedom! Oh, freedom. These freedom seekers wanted to be held by the nameway and the dreamway, who said to us, "Let us share the world and its waters and its sustenance," but they did not keep their promise. They just made shapes with their mouths and drew pretty pictures and wrote dictionaries—lists of words so they'd understand us and learn how to better fish in our sea—and all of them sang and shared bodies and argued and fished the sea together, and that was freedom.

Within five generations, the fish were gone, and the sea was poison, and our people began to hunger, but these nameway and dreamway just shrugged and retreated to land. And even though they had taken our waters and poisoned them, these siltway of Stone and of Song—these people like you—still wanted to trust.

"We will fix it," they said, "together with our nameway and dreamway friends," but why would their friends want to fix that which did not threaten them? You'd think the nameway and dreamway peoples would be content with our destruction, but now that the sea was bitter, they began to destroy the dry land. They fought with each other and poisoned the rivers, and war broke out everywhere. The fish were gone from the sea and we fought them for food, and we fought each other. The whole world suffocated on its own stench in the end. The ancient Shoal was torn apart— sunk—destroyed. Five hundred generations—five hundred generations!

Those of us who refused to bond with outsiders, we formed a splinter Shoal. "All together," we promised, "held by each other and for each other, equal in unity, resolute in our togetherness." *Warriors of Stone and singers of Song had led what remained of us out of that burning world—out on Bird's feathers and through the void. But then they wanted to trust another nameway, to fall into his hands. As if nobody learns anything. The collective must not separate. Must not defect. Must not betray. There is no safety outside of the Shoal. There is no freedom for a single person if that endangers the Shoal. There is no freedom for the Shoal beyond its own survival.*

You must not separate from the collective.

A single person is nothing.

There is no freedom.

Only the Shoal.

I felt the pain as the Bonded Shoal tore into me. It was the pain of true dying—the pain of being severed. I recognized it from before with Old Song, but this was much worse. My bond with Old Song had been newer. The bond with my parent, the bond with my dead, the bond with the Shoal was something I always had. To exist without it was unthinkable, even for a short time before my physical death. My old name was torn away from me too and I was completely alone, floating like an agonized speck of dirt within the Shoal of the dead. Somewhere above me, my body was drowning.

A song of red surged in my dying vision, a song of despair and promise, a song of anger, a song like a light that still beckoned. A deep, resonant voice echoed in my mind, calling me to him even though I was severed— or maybe precisely because I was severed. An orphan. Stone Orphan.

Around me, the prisoned ancestors behind their bond-bars began to chant. I did not understand what they were saying because I was dying. Despair battered me, pain and despair as the Shoal picked my spirit apart, but the ancestors' chant coalesced into *Away. Away. Away. Away.*

I touched the red song. A rope, spinning toward me from an unknown person I could more feel than glimpse at a great distance. Someone solid and resolute. Someone whose light was the color of blood.

I understood the words now. These words, spoken to the Star of the Shoal by a nameway starkeeper called Ladder. The Shoal had rejected him, but nothing truly dies in the Shoal. Within it, in this airless deep, his words still lived on.

"Come to me."

I knew—though I am not sure how—that I had to collect my body. The effort of it almost ended me, but I felt myself—body and soul—an agonizing, disjointed, dying, bewildered whole. I tugged on the red rope, and flickered toward that presence.

In a new place

Later I learned that we all get our first view of Ladder. His age, first of all—different people see different
things. His severe disposition. The light of his candle.
His judgment.

I got none of that, because I landed at his feet, gasping
and sightless and vomiting water. He must have decided
I'd had enough, because I felt him hurting me, worse
than anything I had experienced in the Shoal.

The pain he gave me made my body whole.

He taught me his language, later, word by word, as
he taught me his body, and mine. He was his daily self
then, his regular age. Forty-five, he says. It never changes.
Except when you look at him for the first time.

Ulín looks uncomfortable.

"Why are you upset?" I ask her.

"He hurt you, and . . ." She does not look at me.

"You mean the sharing of bodies." I am suddenly

angry at her. Does she think me a child? "Do you think I wasn't consenting because I was new to his world, to your world of nameway and dreamway? You think I cannot desire because I am from the Shoal, or because I was torn from the Shoal, orphaned and thrust in this new world of yours?"

Ulín seems oddly encouraged by my vehemence. Still, her voice is careful. "You said that the body is not that important for the siltway people. Sharing bodies—the meaning of it might not be the same as here. I was worried that he—that he used your newness."

"Ah." I sigh. "And if I was new to your ways, you think I could not be consenting?"

She bites her lips. "I overstepped. I'm sorry."

I ignore her. "Have I not told you about Old Song, and the stag woman?"

She nods.

I say, "I, too, wanted what Old Song found."

I wanted to feel her passion. I wanted to learn this word *woman*, to understand what it had meant for Old Song, what it might mean for me. I wanted to share the body without the thought of producing new bodies. I say, "I wanted to share the body and not let it be for the common good of the Shoal."

Ulín hesitates. "So you consented . . . as a rebellion."

"I consented, out of curiosity, and yes, newness, and yes, as a rebellion. You cannot deny me this. I am not a child. I am other than you, but I am, and I choose, and become, and this, too, is mine." I do not regret it. Ladder shared his body with me to teach me, and it was work in the end, but it wasn't work for the Shoal.

"I understand," she says, even though I see that it still troubles her.

I speak on, callously. "He taught me to sink into the world of the body. All the things I need for this work." He taught me how to sense skin and wind, how to perceive the world with my magic. To look out of my eyes, in a way no siltway does in the isles, with a gaze that enumerates and accounts. The eyes teach the body how to pass unnoticed, how to perceive people by heat and by magic and how to bypass both, readying for the perfect strike.

I say, "He taught me how to take pleasure."

Ulín looks away. The notebook at her knees lies open, forgotten.

"Did your serpent prince not teach you this? You were new, too, and he wasn't, and your body was not needed for production."

She rubs her eyes. "Most people . . ." she says. "Even your siltway people, it seems . . . most people in this world choose passion. I used to think I did, too. Maybe. I no longer know. Back then it was new, and I was new, and I thought—I loved him, you see, and I thought it would feel better with time."

It's my turn to look away now. "I made you sad. I did not mean to. If you want, just name your target, be it your lover or your brother, and we will come to a deal, or not. This has been painful enough."

"There is no end of pain in my story." Ulín speaks slowly, as if reciting a line from a poem. "The pain is a maze that brought me here, singing with red, calling from under the earth."

I think I understand. She is a client, but also she isn't. She came here because of that voice, the song of despair which is Ladder's to command, but which does not always come from him.

I tell her the story I heard from Old Song and gleaned from inside the Shoal—the story of the siltway Star, of how it fell. "The Headmaster did not catch the star he chose first for himself. His first choice was the Star of the Shoal—but our star denied him. Only I, Stone Orphan from the Stone storyline, came here." I was severed, and if I remained the same, I too would know only this grief, only pain, an endless and incomprehensible maze. But I translated myself. "Ladder trained me. It was a fair deal. But I am still an orphan. Held in a bonded collective with nobody, just like your people."

Ulín speaks, each word as slow as a falling stone. "I am not an orphan, but everything ended when my deepnames were destroyed."

Ulín's brother was prisoned in his rooms, and she was prisoned in hers just as surely, with bandages and blankets and words of care. Healers came and went. Her head felt like a brazier of coals, sputtering and flickering and burning down her throat and out of her eyes. In and out of consciousness. Healers came—in her moments of clarity, Ulín saw them hovering over her. Heat—she could no longer see magic—but heat from the applications of other people's deepnames, and after that, pain. Kannar, her father, hovering behind the physickers, his tall frame stooped and his face sick with fear. His eyes sliding off Ulín's face, never directly looking at her.

She fell back down into darkness.

One time Ulín came to, and her parents were arguing.

She had not seen Sibeli there before, but now they stood at the foot of the bed. Sibeli's face looked bloodless. Ulín wanted to cough and to speak, she wanted her parent to touch her, but Sibeli stood motionless, their hands clasped behind their back. Their eyes on Kannar. His face was livid. So focused were the two of them upon each other that neither noticed that Ulín was awake.

"Day after day she is here, sedated out of her mind by your healers." Sibeli.

"The physickers will help. Someone will know something—some remedy—some hope—" Kannar said.

"Let her wake. Let her recover. Let her—"

Ulín slitted her eyes, pretending to sleep.

"Recover?" Her father half-whispered, fighting for quiet and losing. "She cannot recover without her deepnames—she cannot inherit—"

"Nameloss can never be repaired," Sibeli said, their voice bone-tired. "But she is alive. Let her live."

"Let her live?" her father roared. "Next you will say . . ."

"Kannar." Ulín's parent pointed, and both looked at her, waiting for her to awaken, but she made her breath even. After a while, they resumed in quieter tones.

Kannar whispered, "War is going to break if she is not healed. And even if war is avoided, I have no idea if I'll ever allow her to go back to these—"

"It will be her decision," Sibeli said, quietly.

"The whole of the Coast!" Kannar's whisper came hoarse and furious. "For four hundred years we had peace with the serpents until that son of yours killed three of Laufkariar's cronies that he was always running around with, and now—"

"He is your child too," Sibeli said.

"That murderous snake is no child of mine," spat Ulín's father. "He can rot in that room. Ulín—I need to heal Ulín, I need to fix her, to teach her, I need—"

"Let her wake," Sibeli said. "Let her decide if she is to be subjected to more and more of these healers of yours, or recover and live."

"If not for your insistence on her *free will*, she'd never prepare to marry and never go down to that shore, she'd still be uninjured—"

"It is her will that matters here," Sibeli said. "Ulín is not a child."

"She is—she is nineteen—unformed—" Kannar's hoarse whisper was lost now in angrier, louder tones.

"You are confused." Sibeli, too, was losing their customary calm. "In your anger and grief you call your fourteen-year-old child a snake, and your nineteen-year-old adult daughter a child, and neither—"

"Shut up," Ulín's father roared. She felt a wave of scorching heat, as his deepnames activated—Ulín could no longer see them, but the room became suffocating, as if the air was burning, just like that morning on the shore. "Shut up!" he yelled. "Shut up!"

"No, I will not," Sibeli retorted. "I will not allow you to torture her without her consent—Ulín must decide what she wants—"

Ulín's father's face contorted, and she screamed—*stop it, stop it, stop it*—because she knew what was coming. His power of three single-syllable deepnames—the Warlord's Triangle, the most militant, potent, unyielding configuration in the land—would destroy her parent's deepnames just as her brother had destroyed hers. Ulín screamed and screamed, and the world faded into the tearing blind wail of the headache.

It took Ulín many days to fully regain her mind.

Physickers and healers and nursing people came to the room, talking between themselves. In time, she learned that her parent Sibeli had left—just up and left. She heard whispers that Kannar had struck Sibeli, and whispers that he only threatened to strike them; that he was grieving. She heard it said that Sibeli abandoned their duty to their spouse, to their children, to the Coast. She heard that by leaving, Sibeli did the right thing, and who wouldn't do the same in their place?

Ulín woke up to more physickers, and drifted to sleep again. Her parent never came back. And she could not leave.

"Wait," I ask. "Is it your father you want killed?"

She is silent. I am becoming adept at her silences now.

Three deepnames—not just any three, but a Warlord's Triangle; and he was some kind of leader, a politician, he would be well protected even without his own magic. Still, I would take this on.

"I'm willing," I say. "If you name him as target."

Ulín chews her lips. "Sometimes I do want to kill him. More often than I would like. Rage rises like bile, this memory of unfreedom, but also . . ." She sighs. "More than his death, I want—my father back, the way he was before. Before he stopped seeing *me*, and began seeing *nameloss*."

He stopped talking to her. Stopped listening to the stories Ulín found in books, stopped looking at her comparisons of vocabularies, stopped laughing, stopped taking her on moonlit walks in the quince orchards, stopped gifting her bottles of ink, stopped talking to her about the history of ancient wars, stopped being anything but the procurer of healers. Ulín was no longer a daughter, but a problem that demanded to be solved, before she could be allowed to be a daughter again.

"First you will be cured," Kannar said. "Then we'll party. We'll talk. We will travel to the capital together and go see the splendid singing performances, and the shows of spun glass, and we will drink bad Katran wine and you'll go to the governance sessions with me. You will see! You are not broken, not irreparably." But the corners of his mouth turned down, and his eyes were shrouded. Ulín begged him for a reprieve from these healers, but he only said, "Don't give up so easily. We must keep looking for hope."

I interrupt. "Are you sure you do not want him killed?"

She laughs, bitter. "Between people who see me as powerless and needing protection, and people who see me as broken and needing repair, I have lived these years unseen. But I am a language scholar, and I do not need deepnames in my work. My work stands on its own merit. This is what I want people to see when they look at me."

I regard her levelly. I say, "I see you." I think, *I do not fully understand this language work, but it compels you and always has. You travel widely, and you make friends because you listen. You are brave and learned, and you need neither protection nor fixing.*

"It has been a long time," she says. "A long ten years."

After a moment I lean forward, brush my hand against hers. It is not the clasp of before, no longer desperate or even new. This touch I'm giving because I choose to. "Tell me how you escaped the healing room."

Ulín had tried, surreptitiously at first, to slip out when nobody was watching, but somebody was always watching. She was guided to bed, and her father would appear to scold her. His eyes grew more and more sunken, his wrinkles became deeper, and his anger faster to flare. Ulín thought that his condition was caused by her insubordination, expressed in small ways. It was a few weeks before she found out that the whole of the Coast was experiencing nightmares.

They finally told her what it was. Serpents. Dreamway shapechangers who hunted the Coastal people in dreams, chasing them through watery depths of horrors unknown. Some of her kinspeople dreamt of being torn apart, being devoured. Some never woke up from such dreams. Others sickened.

It had been hundreds of years since her people had quarreled with the sea-serpent people, even though peace was often uneasy—but now the Coast was preparing for war. Across the garden-grown land of the Coast, those magically strong were gathering in groups and in councils. The Coast had been a part of the Katran Oligarchy for centuries now, and paid tribute to the Governance, but their Katran overlords would offer them no support. Still, the Coastal houses were rich in named strong. And Kannar was home. In the Katran capital he served as a minister of war, and his Coastal fighters were powerful and hardened. From the capital, too, he summoned even more healers, more callous and ruder by far than the ones at home. Ulín spent most of her days floating in dreamless sleep. It was something they put in her drinks, and no matter how much she would spit them out, these people with power over her were everywhere now, and she had no deepnames anymore with which to resist them.

She never saw the dreamway nightmares. In her hours and minutes of waking, Ulín thought it must have been the drugs they gave her.

But then, one night, Laufkariar came. In serpent-shape.

He leapt from the dreaming wilds, slithered down from the ceiling, deadly and glinting with scales. Around them, the great house was quiet.

Ulín's head was pounding. There was magic happening somewhere, and she needed to think, but then Laufkariar shed his serpent skin and stood before her in a man's likeness. And oh, he was beautiful like this, his bare skin gleaming iridescent green in the light of the stars that pinpricked his arms and bare shoulders, and his bluish-green hair was studded with pearls.

He smiled, that smile that Ulín had thought she had forgotten. She forgot everything else then, her hands reaching up to his shining.

His kiss cleared the drugs from her blood. Even the headache receded. But she still could not think. Only feel.

When he broke the kiss, he spoke. "I have asked for your hand in marriage, and I still want that. A condition of peace between your people and mine. I will call my fighters back from the vast dreaming sea, and your people's nightmares will end. Your brother's crime even will be forgotten. A bride, a wife, you will live with me underwave. Our child—and we will have a child—will inherit both kingdoms. It is a good deal."

He did not say, *I love you.* He did not say, *Do you want a child?* She thought about it only later, how he asked her nothing at all about what she wanted.

"Did you want a child, Ulín?" I am curious, but there is a sadness to it. I add, "Perhaps, like me, you did not want *production.*"

"This is not how my people think of it." But she

thinks of it now, her face hesitant, suddenly unsure. "See, a thousand years ago when my people were new to the Coast, our foremother Ranra asked everyone who was able and willing, to give birth . . ." She chews her lips. "Is that production? We were so few, and newly escaped from disaster that befell our archipelago."

"So everybody gave birth."

Ulín says, "Not everybody. People still had a choice, of course. But—everybody understood the need."

"In the Shoal as well. Our siltway people, too, were so few, newly escaped from disaster. There's still not enough people. It is a duty to the collective."

"Ranra called it a rekindling. But it is seen as a duty, yes." Ulín shrugs. "Nobody can force anybody to give birth. Some people want children, others don't. But this was a different thing. Laufkariar wanted—it was a political plan he had. Perhaps that, too, was a duty to his people. I am not sure."

"I think that what hurt you was different," I observe wryly. "Your lover—he came there to save you from your father, who wanted to save you from your brother, who wanted to save you from your lover."

Ulín's eyes glisten with water. "I just wanted to be free. To be myself."

"But you had been drugged and physicked against your will, and your thoughts were not clear. And nobody asked you what you wanted."

She says, "I did not want to live underwave forever, bearing children and going nowhere, but I did not want to stay in the healing room. And, to be honest . . . I still wanted his touch. Not in bed but . . . his closeness. Was I consenting? I don't know, Stone Orphan. I thought I was."

It seems clear to me. "You were drugged. He did not ask anything."

"All my people now hated his people. I refused to hate his people, or him, or—it was all wrong, and I could not figure it out. So I went with him."

I do not offer my hand this time. Ulín is curled upon herself, almost crushing the notebook on her knees. I say gently, "The people who should have loved you had hurt you. There seemed no other place for you to go. To be. To be safe."

"Is that consent?" she asks me hoarsely.

"I would call it survival."

Laufkariar took the serpentshape and wrapped Ulín in his golden-green coils, and he carried her up into the dreaming wilds, into the vast violet sea full of movement and terror.

It was the worst thing yet. Suffocating and purple-gray and full of menacing slivers of bone, and nothing to breathe. She screamed in terror, and he bit her at the base of her neck, and she could not move or scream anymore.

He brought Ulín back to his home. To his rooms.

He took the personshape.

He put her into his bed.

"I am so sorry." My hands are clasped in my lap. I brace myself not to reach out. Touch is not what Ulín needs right now, I am sure of it as I am sure of anything.

I wonder how can someone so eloquent be silent so much. I want to take one of these notebooks and write a dictionary of her silences.

I say, "You do not need to tell me. I will not pry. I assume it is him you want killed. I will do it gladly."

I have the skills for this. Surviving underwater is easy. The dreaming wilds are not a danger to me. When my dirk sinks into his neck, I will smile.

She pries her mouth open to speak. "He never forced me."

"All right." Not much of a defense of him, but I am relieved to hear this.

Laufkariar sat on the edge of the bed. Ulín was still paralyzed, but she could think. He was so beautiful, and she knew that only the First Dreamer could have carried her whole body through the dreaming wilds. He made no move to caress her, but he seemed almost drunk.

"I am the most powerful dreamer in the west," he said, and his voice was pleasure and power. "Nothing can stand between me and my heart's desire, not even your brother. Especially not him. I heard that your father imprisoned him for hurting you. Well, I'll do even better. For hurting you, my bride, my wife, your brother will die. I had seen your father's dreams, and I'm sure he will love me for it, and if not, he will understand me.

Perhaps we will even be friends. Then will your brother's crime be truly forgotten."

Wait, Ulín wanted to say, but she was paralyzed.

I grimace. "What would you have said if you hadn't been paralyzed?" I imagine her saying, 'Please don't hurt him, this is *my* revenge. One day I will travel to Ladder's court and hire an assassin.' I swallow hard. I waited so long for my final graduating contract, and now that she's here I am bitter. Her story upsets me more than I am willing to show. "Forgive me."

"I would have asked for peace." She sighs. "Or perhaps I would not. I was only nineteen, and so hurt. But I hope that I would have asked him for peace. In any case, I could not."

Laufkariar did not wait for Ulín's voice to return. And she knew full well that he did not think these decisions were fit for women.

He laughed when he took the serpentshape and leapt up to the dreaming sea, leaving Ulín in the bed, still unable to move.

A few hours later, she regained her voice, and her limbs were just beginning to thaw when Laufkariar crashed from the dreaming wilds and into the room.

Gone was the grin and the triumph and the gleam. His serpentshape sloughed off him. He was badly wounded. Torn, slashed, and bleeding. Something was wrong with his face.

"What happened, love?" she asked, but when he looked at Ulín, she saw only his hate.

"Your brother might be out of my reach, but you are here," he snarled. He took a step forward, but then his people ran into the room and began to fuss around him.

His rage was cold when he hit her later that night, for the first time.

I hiss. I am not supposed to feel this fiercely about a contract, but I don't care. "You waited ten years to purchase this assassination. Perhaps you were short on money? Don't worry. I'll do it for free."

"I have money," she says quietly. "But . . . I still do not know if it's Laufkariar I want killed. He didn't—eh." That *eh* sound she makes is so achingly familiar, I need to tell her—

She rubs the sides of her face. "I am sorry, Stone Orphan. Could you—could it be your turn now to speak? There's—too much despair."

I shrug, pretending calm. "You've come to the right place with your despair. I can tell you about serving despair."

The lore of assassins

When I came to Ladder's court of sandstone terraces, I did not know where I was or what it meant. I was severed and bleeding, having narrowly pulled my body out of the siltway isles through an age-old memory which wasn't a bond in any way that I knew. Instead of the cold, wet spray of the sea, I felt heat under my hands and knees, and a burning in my throat as I coughed up water and bile.

The Headmaster chose not to kill me. I did not yet understand that he could, and that it was a choice he had made.

When I stopped throwing up and I lay in a small sandstone cave where a pool of water was poured for me, I experienced hope for the first time—a feeling of sweetness under my tongue. All colors brighter. A quiet but persistent melody. I was an orphan now, but in a place of orphans—this much I understood. This place, I thought, would be different from the Shoal. A place where nothing watched you from underneath. A place of warm earth, like Old Song's tales of the forests of Lysinar, where small multicolored flowers grew like a carpet in the glades. A place where orphans came for refuge.

Nothing much grew here—not even moss, and the colors of green and mist were replaced by the scorching of sun—but I accomplished what I had wanted. I had traveled toward your people and their lives, like those old warriors of Stone and singers of Song who wanted to travel—and I was no longer imprisoned in the Shoal. I was free.

I met other students, too. Most were much younger than me, a few barely children. Some were my age back then, or older still. They lived separately from me. At first, I thought it was because they did not need water to breathe at night. Later I learned that they roomed with each other, ten to a room in the first circle of training, but nobody had wanted to share with me.

Back then, I wasn't bothered. I reckoned I'd meet them all later, when I learned the language well enough to converse. I did not know yet how many students die in the first circle of training.

He was patient with me, Ladder was. And I wanted to learn. He taught me the ancient ways of the Stones.

"Was this when you became lovers?" Ulín smiles at me. It's a small, tentative smile, but it's there, as if she wants to show me that she has accepted my words from before. That I chose this, of my own free will.

I tell her, "No, that was later. And that word, lovers, it is wrong. He is the Headmaster—there are things he can only teach through his body. You would understand if you chose that path. You heard his song, like me."

She shudders.

"You do not want to become an assassin—or is it that you do not want to share your body?" I ask her.

She is silent again, and I regret pushing her after she tried to be kind. I say, "You do not need to answer. I will continue."

The ancient ways of the Stones are the ways of warriors. It was easy and joyful for me to learn how to move my body to avoid and trick my enemies, how to move soundlessly, how to identify the points of attack, how to strike and to kill, and yet never be sullied with blood. To learn all these skills, he taught me the nameway language, too. Verbs. I did not understand, at first. To move. To strike. To kill. To fuck. To be.

This I understood later—verbs are motions. You *move*, covering *ground*. You are a *figure* on this *ground*, just you alone against the backdrop of the landscape. Both nameway and dreamway people think this way, the exact same way. The magic might be different, but the minds are the same. The nameway and dreamway are *the same*. Bondless. The siltway people do not need to talk so much about motions, because we have bonds. We flicker along these bonds, from self toward other, from where the self is toward where the other is. Landscape is not important. When one is alive, the land is hardly noticed. Dead, it does not exist—just the waters in which the Star of the Shoal floats forever.

But the nameway and dreamway people are all orphans. So you pay attention to limbs, you shuffle your feet over rocks and sand and forest glades, hoping perhaps at the end of this journey to see another person, but that's only sometimes the case.

Haltingly, when I could, I asked Ladder about death. "When we leave the body," I said, "we simply move to the Shoal. The just-dead ancestors are closest to the isles, but as generations are added, we sink deeper. Souls are bonded in life and in death, and there is almost no difference. Where do your people go when you die?"

He grimaced. "The goddess Bird takes most. Where she takes them, I do not know. If you had three deepnames, you could see her coming for the souls of the dead—each person sees her as a different Bird. I saw her once as a raven."

I thought about it as I lay alone in my sandstone cave, where the water kept getting shallower from heat no matter how much I added to it. That night I dreamt of a presence beneath me, a vast globe made entirely of embers that burned so brightly. Then it ashed over into darkness. Again and again the red embers flickered and faded, and I was filled with despair. A sense of vast beauty and also meaninglessness, like nothing mattered in the end. No matter how I tried and how much I learned, the burning coals would wink out into bitter flakes of ash. And the song was coming from them, a song I recognized.

I thrashed in my cave, suffocating in the too-shallow water. I was foolish to think I was free, that there was no presence underneath. This was like the Shoal, only worse—all red and forever dying.

Below, I asked Ladder in the morning. "What is there, below?" My speech in your language was still halting, see.

"Ah," he said. But he did not explain yet.

When he was ready, he made me spar with the others. He taught me how to gauge an opponent's intent from the tells of their body, but I found it easier to trace the patterns of heat. Bodies are unimportant, but bodies are what I focused on now that I had no family and no afterlife, and I noticed all kinds of things. Bodies were motion. I, too, moved against air, making minute sounds and changes as I moved. If you notice how heat wraps around bodies, you can predict how motions will go.

I did not notice any of that in the siltway isles. All we looked at was bonds. And the magic of deepnames, too, we used only for bonds. All we noticed was our togetherness.

Here, my two deepnames served me as weapons. Assassins take balanced deepnames—one and one syllable, or two and two, or three and three; I was unbalanced between my one-syllable and my two-syllable, but my magic was powerful and fast when I wanted to strike.

I killed my first person on the training grounds.

"Don't look at me like that," I tell Ulín. "I am an assassin."

She looks abashed. Did she forget that she wanted to hire me?

I say, "We slay each other in training. This is normal." Although I am not sure what normal means anymore.

"This is expected."

She nods, as if unconvinced. I go on.

When I killed for the first time, Ladder praised me, but all I wanted to see was the goddess Bird coming for the soul of that nameway youth I defeated. But instead I sensed something else. That vast presence under the ground—a star, as if made entirely of coals—reached up, and caught the soul as it tumbled away from its bodily shell, and pulled its ember underground.

Yes, the soul was coal, ignited by the fiery presence into a great brightness as it sank deeper in my vision, deeper toward the fiery darkness, the abyss.

Ladder smacked me on the arm, and I shuddered.

"Don't look." He said, "Not yet. I will tell you when."

It took a long time before I was ready.

I stop, and inhale. "How about you tell me something now. How you escaped."

"Give me a minute," she says, her voice unsteady. "I need to stretch my legs."

"I will make us more tea." I eye Ulín with concern as both of us get up. She seems shaky.

She says, "I'll be all right. I have traveled widely. I am strong." She sounds unsure, but she stretches with determination, as if it's a job that needs her focus. "A bit more, and I can begin."

At last, a choice

Every night, the prince of the serpents returned to his chambers in a foul mood. Ulín pleaded with him not to hit her, and sometimes it worked; sometimes he told her he had never hit her, that she was lying, that he had always been gentle and loving. After all, he had taken Ulín in after her father kept her drugged and bedridden, useless to him as a daughter unless her deepnames came back. But Laufkariar did not need her deepnames. In fact, he preferred her this way.

And he still gave her gifts—not any less lavish than before—strings of pearl and garments of sewn silver scales embroidered with minute flying fish. He gifted Ulín caskets in which to keep her new treasures, and bracelets—even though she tried to refuse—bracelets that jangled and distracted her when she tried to write in her notebook.

When Laufkariar left for the hunt or for council, Ulín would go out and talk to his people, her language skills building for her a bridge. Most of the people who talked to her were other women, of high rank and yet not as powerful as Ulín thought they should be. They showed her the libraries and the gardens in the palace underwater, the vast rows of pearls cultivated in their shells, and the sea vegetables which had to be harvested in the water outside. These women exchanged words with Ulín, and she listened eagerly to their stories, and was careful with what she wrote down.

She made friends—none too close. They all were afraid of Laufkariar.

Through whispered stories, Ulín learned that her brother had fought Laufkariar not once, but twice. That first time, when three of Laufkariar's companions perished at her brother's hand, the prince of the serpents came back home wounded. This was just before Ulín's nameloss, she realized. She thought that her brother had been in a fight.

But she dared not ask Laufkariar what happened. She never did find out.

When Laufkariar made love to Ulín, he was gentle, but she no longer had deepnames, and so could no longer control her fertility; and there were no herbs and potions here that she knew.

So Ulín begged her women friends for such herbs, and gave her treasures away pearl by pearl to pay for these remedies. She was careful, but he found out in the end.

Laufkariar did not hit her that time. It was his words which wounded her more.

His voice was hot and scalding, but his eyes were cold. "Your vermin of a brother might have locked off the dreaming wilds above your land, and we have made a truce, but you are the thing I have bargained for, and you are the thing I will have. I have not forced you—be grateful—but we made an agreement. My child in your womb. You are nothing otherwise. Who will want you? Your father? Your brother? Don't make me laugh. You are alone—magicless—here, in my power, under the wave—you have nothing except for my favor. Nobody else cares about you. Nobody."

Ulín wished he'd killed her, right then and there, but he did not. And she was not allowed to leave the room anymore.

Why does she hesitate about this target? I do not understand. "I can swim underwater," I tell her. "I bet I swim as well as this prince of yours, if not better. He might have his serpentshape, but I have gills and my training, and if the Ra—if your brother could fight him off at barely fourteen, I can kill him."

Deep in her story and her pain, Ulín does not notice that I have almost misspoken. I cannot keep this up much longer.

Ulín shakes her head. "I am unsure."

"I, too, am unsure—unsure why you hesitate."

"Maybe if you hear more," she says, but she herself does not sound convinced.

Laufkariar's sister visited Ulín one day, when he was out. When she rattled the door with her key and stepped in, Ulín thought the other woman was alone, but others came at her heels. Laufkariar's sister looked older than her age and weighed down with sorrow, but Ulín knew the language well now, and they could talk freely.

"This is not right," she said to Ulín, and the others echoed her. "He is my brother, and the First Dreamer of my people, but this is not right. The war has ended. You should not be a prisoner."

Ulín turned to her, beyond tears, beyond hope. "In my room in my father's house I was barely awake for the drugs. Here I'm awake and aware, but alone with myself, not allowed to go out or to choose my future. Neither is what I want."

"What do you want?" another woman asked, a librarian Ulín had come to regard as a friend.

The words fell from Ulín's mouth like hot coals. "I want to be free."

"And you do not want to remain here among us?" the librarian said.

A different woman said, "We may not be able to protect you from Laufkariar's anger, but you should have freedom of movement."

Laufkariar's sister said, "He does love you, you know."

Ulín looked between them all. Six women were here with her, younger and middle-aged, thin and stout, beautiful and plain. Their seaweed hair was elaborately braided and bejeweled, and their garments shone with ornaments made of nacre. They were all noblewomen.

Ulín wondered how many were magicless, and how many could take serpentshape.

One said, "He will be calmer once you give birth."

"I am not planning to give birth," Ulín said, but an older woman, a gardener, looked her up and down.

"As you say."

The gardener's daughter, a young woman close to Ulín in age, looked at her mother in surprise, then gave a small nod.

The others did not notice, but Ulín's hand stole to her stomach.

"You will have to give birth if you stay here," said the gardener quietly.

A child. Ulín never wanted a child. She especially did not want to have a child when she was held prisoner, not allowed to even leave her room. And if she were to leave the room and roam, a child in tow, what future would that be? Ulín had wanted to travel. To learn new words and discover how languages grew among people for generations. She always wanted to go to university. Ulín did not want a child at all, and she certainly did not want a child who would be born against her will, tying her to a place she could not leave.

"I want to leave," she said.

The women talked between themselves and argued, their tones rising and falling, but nothing was decided that night. It was another week, and another day with Laufkariar once he returned, and another evening of pain, before the other women came to a decision.

Three of them came to Ulín's room when Laufkariar was out. He was with another woman, Ulín was told, a woman of the serpent people, but this mattered little to her. On the Coast, her people had their freedom of lovers and lives; such customs were deemed scandalous among the people of the serpents, as was Ulín's indifference to his straying. But now Laufkariar's affair was in her favor—he was not in the dreaming wilds, and he was occupied. The three friendly women—the librarian, the gardener, and the gardener's daughter—took Ulín by the hand. "It is now or never," they said, and she said, "Please, now."

"Where shall we take you?" they asked.

"To my parent, if you can . . . I do not know where Sibeli is now . . ."

They whispered between themselves. All three had serpentshapes, not nearly as powerful as Laufkariar's, but between them they carried Ulín through the dreaming sea while she dangled between them, breathless and terrified and nauseous, all the way until their dreaming powers were spent. Then they emerged in the regular, waking lands, and they swam, carrying Ulín through the cold waves of autumn toward the far shore, underneath the shade of a mountain.

This was North Coast. The mountain was Priadét—this Ulín recognized from her childhood trips with her parent.

The serpent women led her out of the water and to a secluded, small beach, where shells crunched underfoot. "Please take all my treasures," she begged. She had very little with her—a string of pearls, her bag with the useless soaked notebook. "Take what I have left in the rooms." But they shook their heads no.

"Travel far from here, for a while," the librarian said. "The agreements are signed, and nobody wants any more violence between your people and ours, but it would not be wise for you to defy him with your presence."

"We will deal with Laufkariar," said the gardener's daughter. She was putting a brave face on it, but Ulín was grateful.

They embraced her before they left, and Ulín wondered what would have happened if she'd fallen in love with one of those women instead. The gardener's daughter was fierce and proud, and her serpentshape was handsome and strong, and perhaps in a different time she would be the First Dreamer, if women could formally learn dreamcraft and inherit among the people of the serpents, if Ulín's mind hadn't been so set on the stranger she met on the shore. If Ulín had been smarter, faster, older.

"Will I see you again?" Ulín asked the gardener's daughter.

"Maybe one day, when the dreaming sea dreams a storm to my aid, wave by wave she will dream me true."

Ulín did not quite understand, but she remembered, and later, she wrote these words down in a new notebook.

But first she bid farewell to her friends. Then she went east toward the mountain, hoping to find Sibeli.

Sibeli was building a house at the foot of Mount Priadét. It was not yet finished, though the magical structure had been planted and the stonework laid, and Sibeli's people were working now on the house's chiseled wooden trim. It was evening when Ulín found the place, and she could barely distinguish the shape of the house. She was cold and wet and bone-tired, but the wide-open sky and the wind had revived Ulín.

Sibeli ran forward to greet her. They were a tall person, with a stern and somewhat cold demeanor, and they were a welcome sight. They gathered Ulín in their arms, pressed her tight to their chest for a while. This touch was out of character for them, but Ulín clung, reassured by their coolness and their closeness.

Sibeli led her into the house. Even unfinished and undecorated, the sizeable greeting room was warm. Light spilled from magical candlebulbs that floated under the grand wooden beams of the ceiling. Live fire burned in a stone hearth, and for the first time in months, Ulín felt warmer. Her parent's people clustered around them with clothing and drinks, but Ulín begged them to give her and Sibeli privacy.

"Mother," Ulín began.

"Mother?" I echoed. "I thought you used *parent* for in-betweeners?"

"Ah—Coastal speech is not like in the language of the desert. I, too, am translating." Ulín explains, and I think I understand; this word in her own Coastal tongue does not mean that Sibeli was a woman—they weren't—but that the two of them had a relationship closer than any other, and that Ulín was birthed from their body. Only rarely would this word be used, but it was the hour for it.

Ulín said, "Mother, I think I am with child."

"May I?" her parent said. They put their hand on Ulín's belly, and the warmth of their touch told her that Sibeli was using their magic. Then they nodded. "Three weeks."

Ulín swallowed tears, saying nothing.

"He was violent," Sibeli guessed. "I see the bruises on you."

"He never hurt me when we slept together," Ulín said, defensive. "He always asked for my consent."

Sibeli's face held no judgment. "And the bruises?"

Only on other days. Ulín did not know how to say that. *I loved him*—was that even true? *He loved me*—then why did he imprison her, why did he turn violent?

"I am so, so sorry, my child—but it is your decision whether to give birth, and if you would keep it, I will support you."

Ulín looked away. This was the moment of truth. Of her truth. She had loved Laufkariar, but he did not give her a choice to be free. He wanted things his way, only his way. He wanted her pliant, compliant, at his mercy. He told Ulín that he loved her, even after he hit her.

She would be only a womb.

She was more than her womb, and would be now and forever, no matter what her decision would be.

Her parent waited.

Everybody on the Coast understands that children are precious. They are the fragile future of a land that had sheltered her people a thousand years ago, when Ranra brought her ships here, escaping the fire that destroyed the Sinking Lands. Children are an obligation—but lovingly made, raised by parents and partners, and friends and their partners, and kin. Children are also a duty, but nobody can force anyone to give birth. Ulín never wanted a child. She was barely twenty now.

She did not want to make this decision.

Ulín's face is drawn, but her eyes are dry. "I never told this story before. Not even my father knows."

"What would he say," I ask, "if he knew?"

"I have no idea." She is in pain and trying not to show it. "Perhaps he would say to give birth; he wanted a grandchild. Perhaps not to give birth. He hated Laufkariar." She sighs. "Whatever he told me, it would be political."

"Or he would come to his senses, and be your father again?"

A sudden flare of hope in Ulín's eyes is hard to witness. "He never did. He won't. I am not a person for him anymore, at least not most of the time."

"Do you want to stop?" I ask her.

Sadness sits like exhaustion in her limbs, but she says, "There's not much left of it. I will finish."

Sibeli waited. They said nothing, listening and waiting for her.

This was Ulín's choice to make, according to ancient Coastal ways. The person who bears a child within their body has the right of decision. Perhaps Ulín's father would remember that if she reminded him, how consent is always paramount among her people, even though he'd forgotten that in his rush to cure her.

Ulín swallowed bitterness. It did not matter what Kannar thought. Her father was not here. Laufkariar, too, wasn't here.

She was free. She was free.

In a quiet voice, Ulín said, "I do not want to keep it."

"Come with me then," said her parent. "Let us make you comfortable."

A few days later, still nauseous and not entirely well, Ulín was in a hired carriage and headed north to Lysinar.

I perk up. "Lysinar? Did you meet the stag woman there? Her name was Kran-Valadar, Old Song had told me."

Ulín is elusive. "It was a very long journey north in the rattling carriage. Forgive me, Stone Orphan . . . But could it be your turn to speak?"

I am not the only one to keep secrets. I stand up to stretch, then sit down again. I am not happy, but her story was heavy, and it is fair to ask for a rest. I say, "Very well. I told you before how the youth I'd killed became ember and joined the vast globe of coals underground. It happens here, I discovered."

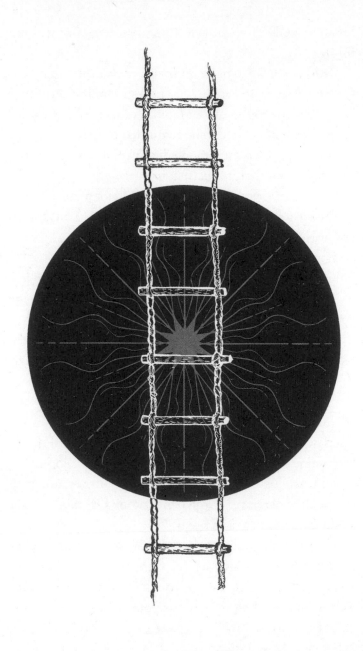

The smoldering heart of despair

Orphans come here, to Ladder's court of sandstone terraces. Some have living parents who exiled or disdained them, yet others had parents who died or were tortured out of their parenting. Some of these orphans have parents whose nature is such that it would be better to be parentless. Some had, themselves, rejected their families. A few had never known their kin. But none of those reasons brought anyone, ever, directly to Ladder's court. It was despair that summoned them.

Some of those who come here, I learned, had committed crimes by mistake. The crimes were unplanned—this is not a place for intentful criminals. But these inadvertent crimes were so terrible that the goddess Bird herself had disdained them, and often their families, and there was no way out of this, no way to live. No hope.

It is despair that makes a person hear the song of the Orphan Star. Its song is yearning and pain. Its song knows you and sees you when everyone else turns away. The song summons you to this court. But even if you survive the training, that despair does not end—you just learn to wield it like a weapon. To serve something greater that makes sense to you, a whole star of despair.

There are three circles of training. First is the beginning, when you are measured against many others, these orphans with grief-deadened eyes. You train and live together in the upper terrace, ten to a room. Many do not survive, but if you survive, Ladder tells you about the body of coal and black shards, the smoldering ruin of star underground which is known as the Orphan.

When the first part of my training was finally done, the Headmaster told me to come at night to the center of the court under the open sky, to the very bottom of the terraces, where there are areas for students to train and to fight. At night, the stones here give up their heat to the cooler desert air. Under my feet, I could sense a faint thrumming. There was something there, underneath.

Ladder's body loomed huge and unrelenting in the semidarkness of the court. His bare arms and bald head almost shone, reflecting the stars, or so it seemed to me. I felt I was dreaming. My vision was full of floating sparks, sudden embers that flared and winked out, and inside me I felt hunger. Like Old Song's melody before we were judged. Such anguish was in it, as if singing, *No way out. No way.*

Ladder took me by the shoulders, a touch which was not that of sharing or teaching, but a command. That, too, I understood in the body. Inescapable, and yet so comforting and solid. I was held.

"Stone Orphan," he said. "I don't know you and you won't be worth knowing, unless you survive to learn. The second circle is when you're tempered. Are you ready?"

"Yes," I said.

He tapped his foot on the floor. A heavy sound.

Something turned underneath, and then I was falling.

Long ago, there was a world in which nameway, dreamway, and siltway people all lived together. They had different countries perhaps, or different continents; they shared big cities and even small islands. The siltway people were guardians of the sea, their deepname magic fishlike, gathering and guarding all the small living beings of the deep. And they fished, too, and as they fished, they made sure that the shoals of the sea would never diminish. *Share with us*, said the nameway and dreamway people of that world. *Let us share the bounty of the sea, and we will teach you what we know of land.*

I was falling between them now. What was left of their world. Coals and embers, tied between themselves in a structure which was not that of bonds. It was spherical, with longer, weaker deepname-souls on the edges and stronger, shorter deepname-souls in the center. They were not bound together in an undulating structure, like the Star of the Shoal, but they clung to each other by some other magic, surrounding a powerful, invisible core I could not quite see.

And all of them wailed.

Lost, all lost. You cannot save a world. Dead forever, hanging in the crucible of ember, dead forever and devouring the souls of the living, for no star can live unsupported by those alive.

I heard among them the voices of the siltway warriors of Stone and singers of Song who had chosen to separate from the original Shoal and join with their dreamway and nameway allies. Their souls called out to me in the siltway tongue, but the way they spoke it was different. I recognized some of the phrases, some of the words, but the structure of it moved and shifted with additions I did not recognize.

Did these kinspeople of mine take bits and pieces of language from their friends, live lives of *figure* and *ground* just like I had learned it?

What good did it do to these ancient siltway? They mixed their language with that of the nameway and dreamway. They lived all together. Together, they ruined their world. Only my people survived, the siltway of the splinter Shoal, the ones who never united with any strangers. They left the dying world on Bird's wings. Our new Bonded Shoal had no ancestors, no masters, no guides. The Bonded Shoal had only each other, only our unity, the single voice in which nobody truly died and nobody was free.

The despairing souls I saw in the Orphan were the ones that united with others. My ancestors were in the Shoal and these ancestors were bound in the structure of the Star of Suicides, the Orphan's heart of despair. All of them, neither alive nor gone.

The Star of Despair, too, needed the living. Ladder's words, so casually spoken throughout my training, finally made sense for me. Not many survive the first circle. The youth I killed, and others, and I myself, all who wailed for their lives to end, but came instead to this court, all of us were nourishment—a shallow layer of living above this ember-shoal of the dead.

What have I done? Despair opened me like I was a shell and settled inside me, smoldering. Twelve stars had arrived in the world in Bird's tail, and all of them were alike. All people, the nameway, the dreamway, the silt-way, all of us lived under the yoke of these ancient and wounded stars. I had simply exchanged one shoal for another.

My despair felt endless, devouring, spilling out of me like ribbons, and in response to that feeling the coals of the Orphan Star flared brighter.

You are one of us now, the voices said.

We are the Star of the Last Resort. Nobody is turned away. All are welcome. All who lost hope.

Send us souls, the voices continued, *souls broken and numb in their grief, souls that are disdained by Bird and others, souls that have no other place to go. The Orphan welcomes them.*

I wanted to fling myself deeper into the star's blazing abyss of soul-embers and nothingness, to dissipate—if I could—to forget—but I stayed, hovering in the darkness, listening to the voices. Some told me their crimes and their stories. Others were silent. For all I had learned about the ways of the body and all the different things that nameway and dreamway people do, death did not mean much here either. It was simply a change of state.

I felt . . . empty, I think. My purpose in the Shoal was to birth, and here, to kill, and all of them meant the same—a transformation into and from the body in the service of a star. It did not matter. Nothing mattered. Hopeloss was ember-fire around my head; my deepnames burned, squeezing and distending me, but I wouldn't know if the pain was real. The pain was no match to what I felt in my heart.

Some time later, I felt more than saw a trapdoor open in the great distance, above. The meaning of Ladder's given name revealed itself then, because he spun a rope ladder out of his magic and threw it all the way down to me.

When he pulled me out to the court of sandstone terraces, still in the darkness, he examined my head first of all.

"The Orphan grilled you nice and well," he began, and I twitched. Was he really—

He noticed my discomfort, and a corner of his mouth lifted up in a cruel smirk. "Be grateful I fished you out."

I swallowed whatever I was about to say. This was his shoal, and he could do whatever he wanted.

The Headmaster continued, "Matched deepnames— feel them for yourself—you now have two two-syllables."

In the School of Assassins, we call this configuration of magic the Dirks. Now I was ready to begin the second circle of training.

"So the name you gave me earlier?" Ulín says, and I know she finally understands.

"That is right. I no longer hold the deepname of *kah*. My single-syllable deepname had been lengthened by the Orphan, so I was in no danger by sharing the old one because it does not exist. What did you think?"

She nods, sadly. "I would never ask for such a secret. But I thought you trusted me."

I shrug. *Not back then. Not completely, even now.* But I don't say it.

Ulín says, "The things you are telling me—aren't those secrets of this school, of Ladder's court? Why do you reveal them to me, especially if you don't trust me?"

"I want to trust you *now*," I say, exasperated. "Listen on."

I was finishing the second circle of training. At this circle, two students would share a room. I was given a room with a pool, and a spare bed intended for someone not siltway, but it was always empty. I had made no friends here—even after I learned the language, nobody wanted to share. I did my first assignments. My tests. Soon I would be ready for the third and last circle and the big assignment—and then, graduation, with it garments of unsullied white made of the magical cloth of bone. Once clad in those garments, I would move all but unseen in the world of nameway and dreamway, accepting assignments on Ladder's behalf. Or better yet, he would sell my contract to a high-powered person, and I would go out into the world as a guardian to royalty. I doubted anyone would be interested.

"Who wouldn't want to buy your contract?" Ladder said. "You would bond to this person and flicker to their side when they need you. A priceless skill."

I did not argue or respond. I did not think I could flicker to Ladder—this was untested after that first time I came to him, vomiting. Even when I was inside the Orphan Star, he extended his ladder to me so that I could emerge. I did not flicker anywhere. The thought of bonding to a new patron filled me with flatness. If ordered, I would attempt it. Maybe.

Those days, the world seemed grainy and thick, like mist. Or like dust, or like sand, or like deepnames, or souls. Some tiny things that go together, clutch each other for warmth, for deliverance, for duty, even for fear. I did as I was told, and when I killed, the souls of my targets went into the Orphan.

Some went willingly into their Star of the Last Resort. Relieved beyond hope that anyone had wanted them. Others had had other desires, but they went anyway. What choice did any of us have? Bird had disdained all of us in the end. She shook the stars from her tail. If she loved us so much to save us, then why did she let us fall?

I was all alone with those thoughts of mine, until one day the round iron gates of the court opened wide—for Ladder to admit a newcomer.

More stubborn even than the stars

Ladder himself stood, as was his custom, in the middle of the roofed greeting space that flanked the gate, his stance wide, and his powerful arms bare. He wore a jacket of old black leather open at the chest, and trousers of leather, and I wondered why it felt like he had dressed up.

What was the occasion? Would-be assassins always came here, bedraggled and starving sometimes, often wounded, woe in their eyes. To come here, they crossed the desert alone, all the changing landscapes of it, the deadly memories of lifetimes never lived, the poisonous creatures, the thirst. If they survived, they came through the gates to see Ladder for the first time. To kneel at his feet. To see his age-changing.

I had missed seeing that when I came here, so I would watch when others arrived, for all the ages of Ladder I would not otherwise see. Twenty-five? Sixty-four? This time, the real surprise wasn't Ladder.

The gates flew open, and a youth appeared.

Unlike the others, he wasn't on foot. He came floating on a carpet. A dun-brown carpet with a faded pattern of flowers. It felt to me for some reason like the carpet was made of sand. The newcomer was dressed in a long, flowing black dress embroidered with black shining thread, pinwheel patterns. His feet were bare. Above his head, numerous deepnames floated like a diamond crown. I could not count them, so blinding they were.

I had never before seen such a sight.

He jumped down, and the carpet dissolved to dust at his feet. I did not then know his grammar, but he told me later that he used masculine forms. And he wasn't all that young, either. In his early twenties, perhaps.

Only then did I remember to look at Ladder.

The Headmaster stood younger, thinner, and angrier by far than I had ever seen him; his fists were clenched. I had seen many of Ladder's ages by now, but never before did I witness him at sixteen. He felt gaunt and murderous. Starving. Unstoppable.

Two other students who came to the gate to witness the newcomer with me now retreated, but I stood my ground. This felt invigorating to me, as if after months of dust I was inhaling a sea storm.

"Who are you?" Ladder asked, more sharply than usual. "Why are you here?"

"I am known as the Raker," the youth replied. His voice was cold and challenging, rearing up to a fight. "I come because you summoned me."

"I did not summon you," hissed Ladder.

The one called the Raker said, "I heard your song. I was having a very pleasant time, but your song disturbed me. I listened to its summons. Now I'm here."

The youth crossed his arms at his chest, and I watched

him stare at Ladder as the Headmaster mimicked the Raker's pose, cross-armed, both of them breathing with a rage I did not understand.

"And are you bereft of parents?" Ladder asked. "What woe brought you out of your *very pleasant time*, to my court?"

"My parents are living. Much good does it do me." The Raker's expression was inscrutable. "I heard that those who commit crimes inadvertent but terrible are summoned here. I am one of those."

"And when you were having your *very pleasant time*, due northwest of here is my guess, with people who hate me and who, without doubt, adore you, why didn't you just stay there where it's oh so pretty and pleasant, and where, without doubt, they sang your praises?"

The Raker averted his eyes. Perhaps, for him, that was equal to kneeling.

He was silent for a while. His jaw moved. Then the Raker spoke, in a flat tone. "I harmed my sister. I do not wish that erased. Those who seek to erase my crime, for whatever reason, are not serving me. They are serving themselves."

Horror reflects in Ulín's eyes, and her mouth opens, but I shush her. "Do not ask me that question. Please wait. Hear my story like I have heard yours."

"If you wish to be served," Ladder said, "you came to the wrong place."

The Raker shrugged. "Every place is wrong."

Ladder uncrossed his arms. "Very well. If you want to learn, I will teach you. But this is not Che Mazri. I will not coddle you. In the first circle of training, you must be prepared to kill at my word, or be killed."

The Raker shrugged again.

I think to get rid of him, the Headmaster gave him hard challenges that very same day. Three students at once, all of them in the first circle, but after months of hard training. The Raker was not prepared to be killed that day, nor was he prepared to tarry. When they attacked him, I saw his rage flare like a blazing explosion in his mind, and he dealt swiftly with his assailants. None were killed that I saw, but neither would they get up.

"What a joke," spat the Headmaster. "Do you think assassination is about beating people up and throwing them about, or flailing at them with your deepnames?"

"Bird peck you to a thousand bloody pieces," said the Raker.

The Headmaster raised his right arm to the sky, and his fist clenched open and close, as if to choke someone high up in the air. "What do you think Bird can do to me? She knows where to find me."

At his command, three more students rushed at the Raker. They were even more experienced, all three armed with dirks and swirling about. This time, the newcomer did not hesitate. It was crudely done, and fast. Three times, the Orphan Star's embers flared and faded.

I expected praise or at least some acknowledgment

from the Headmaster, but he looked as angry as before. "Rage and raw capacity will only carry you so far. You must learn the body."

"If you think I will sleep with you, think again," said the Raker.

"I do not invite you to *sleep* with me, youth. I invite you to study the body."

"I will not submit," the Raker snarled. "No matter what you call it."

Ladder suddenly laughed. "Oh, this is rich. Did my erstwhile lover send you here to try to slay me? Or did you perhaps volunteer?"

"No," the Raker said, too fast. "I came for the reasons I told you."

I did not understand much of this exchange, but I sensed that Ladder had gained the upper hand, the Raker defensive and sullen.

Ladder said, "Go find yourself room among the others in the first circle. I doubt you'll enjoy it, but these are the rules of this court. Work hard, and you will meet the Orphan."

I did not talk to the Raker after that, but I watched him out of the corners of my eyes. He was determined and driven, relentlessly angry and unbeatable. I heard that the others in his room gave him a wide berth, as if they were afraid of him, but I learned from observing that he would wait for others to rush him before striking. He would not attack first.

It took me years to leave the first circle, but the Raker was speedier. Within a few months, in the night, I heard the iron clang of the trapdoor open and close.

The next day, the Headmaster told me that the Raker had perished in the Orphan. "It is a relief," he said, "to have him gone." But his eyes betrayed such agitation that I had to look away. It took four long days for that agitation to settle in Ladder's eyes, and trainings returned to a semblance of normal instead of the previous frenzy.

Deep at night, I was lying in my too-shallow pool trying to breathe well enough to sleep, when the door creaked open. I surfaced, sputtering but ready to strike, but it was only the Raker. He came inside and flung himself upon the spare bed.

"I heard there's room here," he said. "I guess I'm in second circle now."

I did not know what to say. *How could you spend five whole nights in the Orphan Star and come back to the land of the living? I barely survived the one!*

What I said was, "Nobody wanted to room with me before. Are you sure?"

The Raker grunted.

My thoughts churned on. *What did you see when you descended? How did the Headmaster know to extend his ladder to you when he thought you were dead?*

I thought the flatness of my despair would be there forever, but now curiosity stirred within me once more, like a tiny sparkle of sunrise in the wave. I settled for something simple.

"Did the Orphan shorten or lengthen your deep-names?" I asked.

"No," he said.

I sat up in my pool, trying to breathe levelly. There was never enough water here, and it dried out. The transitions between air and water bothered me more than I wanted to let on.

At last, I told him, "Assassins need to have matched deepnames. One and one, Shraga. Two and two, Dirks. Three and three, Garottes. And so on. The star tempers us to this pattern."

"Nobody touches my deepnames."

I fell asleep after that, and slept soundly for the first time in months, even years. When I woke, I saw that the water in my pool was deeper and clearer.

"What happened here?" I asked the Raker.

"You thrash around too much," he said.

Ulín's expression is odd; I cannot read it. "When did you figure out he was my brother?"

I shrug. "When you called him Tajer, a while ago. He shared that name with me, later." Truth is, I wondered even before that.

A look of betrayal flickers in her eyes, then dissipates. "Why didn't you tell me sooner?"

"Would you, in my place?" Perhaps it does not matter if she would. "Our tales were unsheathed together. You told me his story as you knew it, and now I am telling you mine."

That hint of betrayal is in Ulín's voice when she speaks. "Are you trying to make me feel for him?"

I feel frustrated now, too. "No, I'm not trying to make you feel for him. He is not an easy person to feel for, although I'm sure many feel *something*. Do you want me to stop?"

She is silent. In my mind, I have already drafted the dictionary of her silences. This one, I think, is curiosity beyond reason, a desire to know that transcends even pain.

I say, "Very well. Then I shall continue my tale."

That morning, the Headmaster was shocked to see the Raker back in the training court. Ladder's face was motionless, but the corners of his eyes twitched just so, and I had studied his body. If he did not know the Raker was back, if no ladder had been extended to him, then how did the Raker return from the coals of the Orphan Star?

I asked him that question myself later that night.

"You ask too many questions," the Raker said.

"If I wasn't too curious for my own good, I would still be with my people. I would be a part of the Shoal."

"Do you regret leaving?" he asked.

"You ask me without wanting to answer any of my questions. I will trade answers with you, if you wish."

He threw himself upon the bed once more, and turned his face away.

I crossed my arms and leaned against the wall.

Studying nameway bodies came in handy for me then. He would speak first, I knew. He was more powerful than me by far, but impatient; I had him at a disadvantage.

Not too long after he said, without turning to face me, "I answered your question about your pool."

Ah. It wasn't much of an answer. He had spoken up first, as I expected, but only to keep score. He was also right. I had asked him about my pool, and he all but confirmed that he cleared and filled it.

So I answered his earlier question. "No, I do not regret leaving. When I was living in the isles, I wanted to know the purpose of the Stone storyline. Well, I found it. We were warriors once. We encircled our people with protection, and we ventured forth in curiosity toward people and places not our own. We did many things, sometimes contradictory—we journeyed and remained, fought in wars and guarded peace, disrupted and betrayed and led our people to safety. In every story I found where the siltway people took part, there were Stones. I do not regret discovering this. In the isles, we Stones have no purpose."

"Except to rebel," he said.

"Rebellion is not a purpose. Perhaps I do not understand your words."

He sat up on his bed to look at me. At close quarters he looked troubled, with sunken eyes and disheveled hair unraveling from his braid. I did not have a good look of him when he came in at night, and during training I did not spar with him. But now that I attended, he did not look well.

The Raker chewed his lips. "What is rebellion then, if not a purpose?"

"It is . . . I am trying to translate. It is a pushing-away. From one thing, which you are expected to do and to be, you set toward something else." I made a push-away motion. "Studying your language, I understood that a person moves upon ground. But there's more than that. When you push away, you acquire speed, and this speed can carry you past your target. Rebellions move you, not just upon ground, but against and alongside other people. One does not know where one might end up, one is carried, one seeks to have choice and might again lose it."

"You would enjoy speaking to my sister," the Raker said.

Ulín blinks. "Do you enjoy speaking to me?"

I reply, "Maybe."

"I'm sorry."

"No, don't apologize. It is my choice to continue to speak to you."

I contemplate her. Her anger, her discomfort, her confusion. Her curiosity, which is so much like mine. The warmth of companionship we shared earlier. The guardedness of now.

I can stop right here, or continue.

I choose to continue.

I tell Ulín, "I do not love languages the way you do. Studying your language is not a curiosity for me. It is a rebellion. In the beginning, I was all too willing to instigate it, but now I am carried. A story moves back and forth in translation, and it is remade every time. Each of us is a story translated to a language vastly different from its first. You can try to translate yourself back, but it won't be the same story."

After a while, the Raker continued his tale. "I went down to the Orphan wanting to die. The Headmaster thought I was finished."

I waited.

"Nothing can undo my crime. It has no repair. No hope. A person loved me once, back in Che Mazri. They were—they are a ruler of that city. It does not matter."

I waited some more, until he spoke again.

"Ladder said that my lover coddled me. But that's not what happened. It was worse. My lover wanted to cut the bad pieces out of my past, to erase the bits they did not like. My lover said I was too young back then. Too hurt. How could I control myself? Well, I could. And I should have. And I didn't."

I said nothing. If it was a battle, I would be winning.

"I have an excess of power. It is not an excuse. My lover gifted me a net of diamonds to wear around my body. They made it with their magic, so I could constrain my power as needed. At first I thought it a great gift. Then I thought it a yoke."

I did not know the word then. He told me, "A yoke is a rigid harness of wood that binds animals together. They bend their necks willingly to it, but then they are bound."

"What happened to the diamond net?" I asked the Raker, and he turned his head away.

"I threw it into the Orphan."

After a silence, he spoke again. "When I descended to meet the Orphan, I saw myself mirrored. I saw pain and shame unending. The agony of the Orphan Star's birth, which absorbed the despair and the deaths of all its people. The star could have saved them all in the end, but it didn't. Instead, it devoured them. The star judged itself so harshly. Even delivered on Bird's tail, the Orphan Star had little hope. Now it has nothing left. Did you know that Ladder—its starkeeper, its lover, its bonded, its only friend—at the dawn of time desired to catch a different star?"

"Yes." It was too tempting not to share this. "He wanted to catch the Star of the Shoal, but my ancestors who sought his embrace were overruled. And our star escaped Ladder, but not before his gaze was anchored in some of our people. This is how I could come here. The Shoal keeps all generations, and so bonds are eternal in the Shoal."

The Raker looked bitter. "Would you not despair too, if you were merely the second-chosen? I was never the favorite child. Not even a good-enough child. Even before my crime."

"The Orphan gives shelter to those disdained by everyone." This had been a solace for many of us here, and I understood it now.

The Raker said, "But the Orphan, too, wanted something different than to always be second-best."

"And so it called you," I guessed. "Without the Headmaster's knowledge."

The Raker shrugged. "Everybody wants something from me."

"What do you want, then?" I asked, even though it wasn't my turn.

"You ask too many questions."

He turned away and pretended to fall asleep. There was new saltwater in my pool, and it was clear.

Ulín's face smoothed out with my telling, and now she appears calm. "You want me to spare him."

I grimace. "He does not need your pity, and neither do I. I will take on your assignment, whatever it ends up being, and I will be successful. Father, brother, or lover. You are the one with the grievance." I am thinking now, thinking hard about what it all means. An Orphan's contract requires a legitimate grievance. Many have grievances with the Raker, I'm sure, but what if Ulín is the only one whose grievance could bind a contract? And I—what if I am the only one who can actually kill him? It makes too much sense. And I hate it.

I speak. "If that is your decision, I will carry it out."

She says, "I wonder if you are trying to change my mind." And here it is, the steel at her core. She is gentle, but not all that gentle. I am not gentle at all.

I frown at her. "How did you want our conversation to go? You asking me questions about the siltway language and customs, and writing my answers down in your notebook, perhaps some tea, and then you'd pay me for a slaying? Later, you'll write a book about me. *Customs of the Fish People*. I have met people like you before."

"No!" she cries out. "No, Stone Orphan, I did not come here to *use* you!"

"Don't protest." My voice is stone-cold. "It would be easy and pleasant for you to take and take from my labor. No, labor must be done by all. In this, I believe the Bonded Shoal is right. All must contribute their labor for the flourishing of all. So now, you and I are entwined. Not just through the story we shared, but through how we shared it. We exchanged pain and yearning. This was work."

"This was work," Ulín echoes. "The work of the two of us." She is thinking, and I let her be, until she is ready to speak again. "Please, tell me the truth as you see it."

I nod, sharp. "You hesitate. I think you came here hesitating, but now your hesitation is made clear to you through these stories and their pain." Ulín has asked, and so my voice rings with the cadence of the Song storyline. "This is the moment of truth. The moment when a round plain stone is cleaved apart. It is not a regular stone. It is a geode that opens to reveal a cave of amethyst. This is you."

"Perhaps you, too," Ulín says.

I do not deny it.

Ladder called me to his side, the next day. "I heard that you bunk with the Raker. Well, learn his weaknesses then, and learn how to slay him. This will be an asset for your graduation."

Ladder had been disappointed, I think, that I could

not flicker to him as easily as I could when I was in the Shoal. Without my flickering, I would not be such a good prospect for an outside contract. Everything was ashes, but a contract could take me out and into the wider world. Perhaps my contract could even be sold to Lysinar, where I might meet the Kran-Valadar.

So I said yes.

"So . . . you learned how to slay him?" Ulín's voice is hesitant.

I will not allow for emotion. "I've done as Ladder commanded. I'm an orphan and this was my shoal."

She says, "May I ask if you have been lovers? My brother and you."

The things she wants to know are all wrong. "It does not matter if we had been lovers, nor would it sway me if we were." Nor would it be her business if we were.

"Look," I say, irritated. "When I came here, I wanted pleasure in the body. It was not something we talked about in the Shoal. You shared the body for production, not pleasure. I wanted to experience that. But then, the longer I lingered and learned about your people, the more I perceived that the Shoal and this place were alike. I began to want other things." Things like someone who wouldn't use me. Things like a friend.

She says, "Thank you for telling me." I can see Ulín thinking, but I have no idea what she's thinking about. I see her reach the end of her thoughts, and lean back, exhaling. She says nothing.

I tell her, "Listen to something else."

The Raker had a flying carpet that carried him to this court. In the last few weeks, he began to roll the carpet up, and place the bundle under his head when he went to sleep. Sometimes I heard the fabric of it whisper, as if an invisible wind stole into the room, beckoning me to come out to wide-open spaces. It was such a strange feeling each time—not mine, because I never *wandered*. Not like the nameway people wander.

"Where does your carpet come from?" I asked the Raker, one evening.

"What does it matter?" he replied. Then after some silence, "It's sand-made, a carpet of wanderlust called from the heart of the desert by the one with almost no words."

I make myself stop. "Do you want to hear this story? I do not wish to *sway* you, and you do not wish to be swayed. I promise I will take the contract as you choose it."

"My decision is made," Ulín says, and her voice is firm. "I will write the name of the target on this piece of paper and give it to you. When your tale is done, you will read it, and I will not change my mind, so your tale cannot dissuade me."

"It's not my tale," I say. "It is his. And this is how he told me his story."

The Raker's story

I was traveling through the Great Burri desert, the Raker said. I'd been here for a month. An exile. Among the people of the desert, I had already acquired a reputation.

They all wanted something from me—everybody does—but they wanted more from me than my magic. They wanted me to be placating and polite, to smile as I gave what they wanted. When I wouldn't smile, they said I was frightening. They did not like that I did not soften my power. They certainly did not want me to take lovers among them, regardless of what my lovers wanted. I began to stay away from encampments. It stung that they asked and asked for my magic. "Can you make rain? Can you repair this crumbling building? Can you?—Will you?" I helped willingly, at first. But they wanted me to stay only for as long as I was useful. It reminded me of my father. He, too, kicked me out after the truce with our enemies was sealed, and the magical defenses I constructed could be maintained without me.

And then, at the university—they kicked me out too.

I wanted—I wanted to do violence to them all, to pull

their entrails out of their bleeding bellies and relish their screams—but instead I left. Every time.

The desert was not inhospitable to me. When I slept, I dreamt of ruined cities, of round-roof houses of clay, their small circular windows gilded and shuttered with shutters of bone. It was comforting to dream that, but every time I woke up and continued my journey.

One early evening as I was walking the sands, I saw another person approaching. I stopped. I was wary. Desert people tend to travel together, and any trading groups are well-guarded. Was this an apparition? A vision? Someone sent to hunt me?

I called on my deepnames and made a construct of defense. Then I stood there, bristling and warded.

The figure approached me rapidly, but in zigzags, and from the distance I heard a sudden peal of laughter.

It was a youth. No, a child. They were maybe fourteen and almost as tall as me. Their complexion was olive, similar to mine and lighter than most of the people's I've seen here. A crown of dark, loose curls haloed their head, which they tilted to the left side, surveying me with a curious and unwary gaze. They had clothes of bright color—stripes of pink, red, and green—in the fashion of the desert's in-betweeners.

They approached me and stopped, and their eyes tracked my magical structure with wonder, and fearless curiosity. Then they swung their arms, and small, translucent butterflies detached themselves from their sleeves and dissipated into the air.

"Who are you?" I asked in Burrashti, but the youth only tilted their head.

I wondered if they spoke a local language—Maiva'at, or Surun' perhaps—which I did not know, but no matter what words I tried, they did not respond.

I was their age when I committed my crime, but we couldn't have been more different. This child—this youth—they looked so carefree. So cared-for. So trusting.

They reached out, trying to touch the complex, rotating structure of defense I built with my deepnames.

"No," I said, sharply, in my own language.

"No," they echoed in my language, and laughed.

I felt bad, and I did not understand why. So I made a shape for them. It was a bird, a white gull I remembered from my childhood. I released it into the air, where it cawed sharply, then dissipated.

"Butterfly," they said. It was not in Burrashti but in Iyari, a language spoken to the west, in a city which has a cruel ruler. I knew only a little of that language, in which butterflies are called soulbirds.

"I cannot do a butterfly," I told them. A gull was about as peaceful as I could manage. But I thought of Iyar, that springflower city, and I made a vision of flowers—roses I saw in that land as I'd passed it. They were burgundy and dull orange, and beneath their beauty, there was blood.

The youth reached for the flowers, laughing. A thorn pricked them, and they laughed even more and sucked on their finger, while the vision of the roses dissolved.

All of a sudden, they began to dance. I stepped back, giving them space, and they ran around, swinging their arms. Perhaps it wasn't a dance, but there was music in it. They called on their magic. It was unusual, this configuration of two deepnames, each longer and much weaker than mine—a three-syllable and a four-syllable. This was not a configuration of blunt power, and one rarely sees such things in the countries of the Central North, but the youth moved their magic now. It was gentle but sweeping, this configuration that spun like a wheel while the youth now spun too, around and around, pulling threads out of sand.

Then the youth stopped. They waved their hands. The desert's embrace opened for them, and thin long structures of petrified wood rose from the depths of the sandy ground, forming a simple, vertical frame of a loom. Then the thread of sand began to weave itself, while the youth hummed and sang without words. It went on and on, as the sun sank beyond the horizon. I stood there, immovable, witnessing.

When they finished, the loom dissipated into the dying orange light. The youth held out a small carpet.

"For me?" I asked. They thrust it into my hands. Sand, a feeling of motion, and these roses—each petal glowed, and their thorns hung with drops of blood. I rolled the carpet into a thin bundle, not quite understanding the turmoil I felt.

I asked, "What can I give you in return? Do you want—can you even tell me? Do you want magic? Power? Do you want water?"

The youth did not respond.

I dug into a small bag I carried, and offered them treasures I found wandering in the desert—a small, bejeweled scarab beetle covered in ancient letters I could not read, a fragment of cloth woven of silver and beaded with moonstone, a piece of old dried cake I got in the last encampment.

The youth took the cake and was chewing on it when shouts came from the northeast, and a small crowd of angry people ran toward us, their deepname structures blazing in the dusk. There were mostly young women my age; older people trailed them, and at least four lanky and indignant-looking goats.

One of them, a young woman, their leader and seemingly magicless, brandished a spear.

"Kimi! Kimi, come back!! Did he hurt you? I swear, if you hurt him, I will—"

The woman shouted in Iyari, yet others in Surun'. I could not understand much, but gathered that the youth was prone to wandering away, that the angry young woman was the straying youth's older sister. Her lovers and companions trailed her, all shouting of my criminal intent, how I lured the child out to the desert to ravish them. Kimi—that was the youth's name—ran back to their side, laughing and speechless. They would not be able to say anything in my defense, or in their own.

Rage engulfed me. How dare they imply—yes, I was a criminal, but I have never coerced anyone in my life, let alone a person who wasn't of age. I took many lovers, yes, but I would never force anyone. Consent is everything to me.

My rage flared black, and viscous, and endless. With clouded eyes I beheld these people as outlines of heat; all their magic and spears would be as nothing before me.

Something else occurred to me then.

Kimi's sister defended them.

At that moment, my vision clouded with envy and my throat as painful as shards, I saw my futures diverge. I would fight this crowd—kill them all—leave only the youth unharmed. Then I would wander the desert wounded and silently screaming until I came to Ladder's court and threw myself into the Orphan.

Or I could refuse to do violence.

I bit my cheeks bloody before I was done, then turned on my heels and retreated into the desert, my deepnames obscuring my steps in the whirlwinds of dust and the darkening sky.

Only later I realized that I still held the rolled-up carpet. Later yet, I learned that it could fly, not too high above ground, but it carried me.

So I floated southeast, and came to the ancient city of Che Mazri, the capital of the Great Burri Desert, and met my lover.

Everyone wants something from me. Even you, Stone Orphan, even though I'm not sure yet what it is. Except Kimi. I think they did not want anything, that youth with their gaze of wonder who saw only soulbirds and flowers. My lover in Che Mazri certainly wanted something from me, and they made every excuse under Bird's wing to brush away my crime. To cut those parts of me off.

Perhaps my lover wanted to care for me when others would not, but I do not want it. Not like that.

Nobody understands how every moment I must fight myself, how I must guard myself against my own rage, and in this place—Ladder—he feeds it. I told him I do not submit, but he knows me. At his command, I have killed. "To train," he says. "is to learn." Is it right to kill at his command when it's wrong to kill out of anger? He says we kill only the people that the Orphan already marked as its own.

I had sought every lore that meant I would best my enemies and live. But now I ask myself, do I truly want every learning? At what price? My thoughts tangle, dripping blood. So I put this carpet under my head every night, to remember the soulbirds.

"That's it," I say. "That's how he told it to me."

Ulín's eyes are closed when she asks, "How did he leave?"

"Oh, there was a training battle, in the second circle. Students who make it this far rarely kill each other, but Ladder was in a mood that day."

An exit is made

When the Raker defeated his opponent, Ladder told him to finish the job.

The Raker kicked the other student away from him. Looked up at the Headmaster.

"No."

"You will do as I say."

They stood bristling at each other like they did on the day they met. The Raker's fists were clenched. Again he said, "No."

"You are a student. If you are too soft to learn . . ."

The defeated student chose that moment to hoist himself up and launch himself at the Raker, which halted the conversation for the few brief moments of battle. The other student did not get up again, but the Raker still would not kill. And he kept his focus on Ladder. He said, "Call me soft if you must. I don't care anymore."

"You think you've done him a favor by keeping him alive in his shame?"

"Not my problem," the Raker spat.

"I should have known you were hopeless by the company you keep."

"Stone Orphan has nothing to do with this," said the Raker.

"Not Stone Orphan. Your lover in Che Mazri."

The Raker's face twisted in frustration. "You goad me. It doesn't matter. I will no longer kill for you."

"Weakling," Ladder snarled. "Coward."

"Neither," the Raker snarled back. "I restrain myself. By choice. I could have taken your place if I wanted to. Done your job better."

"You think you are better than *me*?" Ladder's voice was rough. "Is that why you're sniveling here and I'm still starkeeper?"

"You keep a star you didn't want, and which does not want you—"

"Sure." Ladder grimaced. "You think you're better? Five nights, and in the end you did not want it at all. Second-chosen or no, I have kept the Orphan Star for two thousand years. What do you think the Court of Despair is about? A big happy family? Dancing and butterflies?"

"Pluck you. Despair is one thing, but you send your assassins after old flames for sport just because you're jealous or bored. I will not be a part of this. I will not kill so that others may devour."

Ladder loomed closer to him, tall and broad and overpowering. "Ah. Is that it? You decided to kill for yourself, devour for yourself—is that why you are suddenly rebellious?"

"Pluck you, not this again," the Raker said, his malice barely constrained. "What I do from now is my choice. I do not owe you or anybody else an accounting."

"You think you're too good for me, for this court? Too good for the world?" Ladder sneered. "Remember what you are. A criminal. Your crime festers. You cannot undo it. And if you—"

The Raker interrupted him. "All my life I was pushed out of places, exiled, kicked out. Well, not here. *I quit.* And I'll take my crime with me when I go. Fix your own Bird-pecked house."

The Raker raised his hand, and the familiar carpet wove itself out of the sand at his feet. I don't know if Ladder would have opened the gate. The Raker's anger flared into a towering structure of diamond, hoisting the carpet and the Raker himself up over the wall of the School of Assassins and away.

In a moment, the Headmaster turned around and his attention shifted to me. I did not see him age-change that first time because I was busy vomiting, but I saw it now. He must have been about a hundred, ancient and just slightly stooped—and absolutely murderous. "Did you learn how to slay him, Stone Orphan?" I guessed from his tone that he wanted to call me names, but this time he desisted.

I nodded. "I did."

"Good." His years slid off him slowly, like moss from a rock, until he appeared again middle-aged. "I cannot send you after him without a contract. We must live by the Orphan's rules, no matter what *he* thinks we do here. But he has a singular talent for making enemies. Someone will have a legitimate grievance. A contract should come soon enough."

Ulín looks slightly nauseous. "So do you think—my arrival . . .?"

"I think so, Ulín. I am sure." I figured it out at last, the Headmaster's plan to summon her here, his plan to set me up with this particular contract. "We were both set up, I think." This was his shoal and he did whatever he wanted.

She is pensive. "This explains why after all those years I heard his song, and was tempted to come here."

"Yes," I say. "But nobody dragged you here. Your anger was all your own. Your grief, your loss, your desire to see justice done for what has been done to you, your disempowerment, your will to make this journey—all yours. This is what made it possible for Ladder's voice to reach you and summon you. This contract is yours. Nobody can force you." He tricked her, but she chose this moment too.

Ulín turns away from me, but her voice is bitter. "I keep thinking, you know, if he was so torn about his crime, he could have at least written me a letter."

What can I say? *Yes, Ulín, he's a mess. You can order him killed and be done.*

She seems to sense the direction of my thoughts. "You can look at my paper now."

"No, it is not yet time," I say, my stubbornness overriding my curiosity. "I concealed things from you, but I think you kept something back too. So tell me about Lysinar."

A miracle at sunset

Ulín sold Laufkariar's jewel-encrusted pen and hired a deepname-powered carriage and a guide. Her aim was to travel north to Lysinar. Her ancestral lands ended with Priadét, and it was all wilderness from there, forests flanking a thin, sandy strip of a coast and between them an ancient trade road, sometimes narrow, sometimes a little bit wider. The land itself was wild here. Small bears fished the waterfalls, unafraid of the deepname-steered carriage and its riders. Birds flew overheard, startled by the rattling of wheels. Beyond the driver and her guide, she saw people only rarely, here and there in fishing and hunting villages.

Once Ulín passed by a bookhouse that stood in the middle of a small town. The building was made of wood and painted lavender, and had books stacked high in the windows. The bookseller was a stooped and ancient ichidi who once lived on the Coast, but had found its gatherings too loud, or so they said. The bookseller had lived in this town now for sixty years, peddling healing herbs and old books that smelled of bitter tonics and honey. Ulín traded more of Laufkariar's gifts for two modest pens carved of alder, and a traveling inkwell filled with walnut ink. She got notebooks bound in leather, and books about Lysini culture and about the ancient war which made the Lysini people who they were. There was also a dictionary of the language of the stag people.

Ulín's journey north from there was a happy one. She read, disdaining the headache for as long as she could; and when the carriage made stops, she jotted notes in her new notebook. The language of the serpent people and the language of the stag people had similar words—words for dreaming and waking, for rain and woman, for hunter and leader and trader. This is what she had wanted all along—this learning, and travel, and wide-open spaces.

She crossed the border of Lysinar, into the land of rivers that gurgled and spoke in the language of water that knows no dictionaries. Birds sang differently here, as if their language, too, was different from what she'd heard at home. Golden mice and voles darted underfoot, their pelts glinting in the rays of sun that stole through the canopy of the great trees. The carriage driver and guide would go no farther, but Ulín did not want to stop. She parted with her companions and walked alone, deeper and deeper into the sun-dappled wood.

It was almost sunset when people stepped out to greet her. Their leader was a woman taller than any nameway Ulín had ever seen. She was proud and regal of bearing, and she was clothed—

I cough, and Ulín frowns at me, but it is indulgent. She says, "Stone Orphan, she was definitely clothed."

I laugh. "Go on."

She was clothed in heavy garments embroidered with the shapes of berries and leaves. Her skin was grayish-green, and her head was crowned in beautiful sunset-pink antlers that branched into the air. These tree-like antlers glowed with the light of hundreds of tiny magical candlebulbs, which must have been planted there by her nameway companions. The people surrounding her were hunters, both nameway and dreamway, dressed in leathers and furs and adorned in ornaments made of brass and beryl and twigs. The queen of these people was unsmiling, but Ulín detected a warmth emanating from her.

"Who are you, and why do you come here, and what do you bear?" the stag woman asked in the common tongue of the North.

She said, "I am Ulín Ranravan, daughter of Sibeli and Kannar, and I am a child of the Coast. I am a person who was named for heirship of my people, but I myself want only words. I want to learn languages, and meet the people who speak them, and share friendship under the open arms of the sky."

The stag woman bowed slightly, and the magical

lights in her antler crown jangled and twinkled, but did not blind Ulín.

"This land does not open its arms to the sky," said the Kran-Valadar, for such was her title, and she was the leader of the hunters and warriors of that land. "Four hundred years ago, my people of the stag were exiled here from Katra. Our star was destroyed, and we ran northwest, where the nameway people of Lysinar welcomed us. These forests grew out of our entwined magics, the powers of the nameway and the dreamway—and all the birds and the voles and the rivers and the lakes. We know what it is to fight and to flee, and we know what it is to lose and to gain. *Friendship* is ever an empty word if no action accompanies it."

"The Katrans attacked us too," Ulín said. "During that war four hundred years ago, after they exiled you, they subjugated our Coast."

"I know this history. Once it was even true," said the Kran-Valadar. "But now your people sit in Katran governance. Your own father is a minister of war. If Katra attacks us, your father will lead the troops. Is this your ambition as well?"

"I do not want power," Ulín said.

The Kran-Valadar heaved a big sigh, and her companions whispered between themselves. "You are still a child," she said. "You have been through much, but you are still young, and naïve. Nobody can escape wielding power. If you have it, you must learn to use it."

"I know what I want," Ulín said, stubborn. "Languages and people and learning. I do not want power. I do not want to choose any sides, to contribute to any wars. I just want to learn."

The Kran-Valadar said, "Once you learn, you change. Once you change, you choose. Once you choose, you exercise power."

"I am powerless," Ulín insisted. "My own brother assailed me and disempowered me."

"You are far from powerless," the Kran-Valadar responded. "But you have suffered and you are afraid, and so you lie to yourself that you're powerless."

Ulín protested, but the leader of the stag people would not hear it.

"Come, I will show you the price of such fear," she said.

She took Ulín to a settlement of log houses on a large forest glade. There was a person who looked different from any nameway and dreamway Ulín knew. This new person was older and fishlike, her skin silvery-blue with scales. Her eyes shone soft silver, and she sang in a voice deep and melodious, sang with words Ulín did not understand. It was breathtaking, that melody, and deeply soothing, and it healed and ruined her heart.

"This is my lover, Beautiful Song of the siltway people," said the Kran-Valadar. "She comes here every few years. She comes here in secret. Her people do not want her to reach out to people not like hers, and she can neither accept her desire nor resist it. We can share the land and the sea, I said to her, but she told me it had been done before, done badly. She told me how it all went wrong. And now she is afraid. Her people, too, are afraid. They hold each other so tightly, so vigilantly, so firmly, so equally, and none of them will ever trust outsiders. They do not trust themselves either, afraid that if they don't hold each other so tightly, the Shoal itself will dissolve. Each fish will go on its own, tossed with the current, powerless and bereft and easily hunted. So they clutch at each other, thinking that it is the only way. But a people can hold together with power greater than fear."

Ulín did not understand this story back then. Not until now.

"Any day now, she'll flicker away from me, my Beautiful Song," said the Kran-Valadar. "But she will return in a few years' time."

"Why do you love her?" Ulín asked, incredulous. "If she cannot overcome her fear and commit to you?"

"She hesitates," said the Kran-Valadar. "That hesitation is her gift to me. None of her people hesitate, but she does. She flickers away out of fear, and comes back out of love. Fear will make her loveless among her tightly held shoal, and love will make her bereft. One day, she will choose. But even now, she is changing. Already she learned the language of *woman* and she chose it, even though her language does not have such words."

I must wet my gills. It is getting urgent, but I am not moving. I say, "This was my Old Song."

"I think so," Ulín says.

"I never heard her other name. This was before I bonded to her."

"I think it was some years earlier."

"All this time you listened to my story, and yet you

said nothing." I feel too brittle to accuse her of anything.

"I wasn't sure at first," she says. "Our tales have un-rolled together, like an ancient scroll from its rod. Un-rolled like a scroll, unsheathed like a weapon. You heard things you did not want to hear, and so did I."

I swallow my feelings. It is not enough. "Old Song had been my teacher. My bonded. My friend. My tormentor. The one who loved me, and the one who abandoned me. If I were a client, she would be the only contract I'd weigh."

"Would you order her killed?" Ulín asks.

"I don't know. Some days, I think I would. Others, I imagine her being brave. I think of her touching me gently, restoring our bond. I imagine her happy with the Kran-Valadar in Lysinar. I imagine her sinking into this word *woman* that suits her so much." I swallow and swallow, but the truth cannot be suppressed any longer. I say, "I imagine asking Old Song, why did you think being a *woman* would ever suit me?"

"Ah," says Ulín. "You are—what you are. Only you can know—"

I interrupt her. "Do you know, when your brother came here, I wondered if he was a woman, too."

I asked the Raker many questions back then. He had been here for months, after all.

I asked, "Why did you not recoil when you saw me? All nameway do. They tell me I look like a fish. They tell me I am uncanny."

He shrugged. "I'm an exile, too."

"Why do you wear a dress, and grow your hair long, and yet use masculine forms?"

He answered, "You don't need to be a woman and I don't need to be a man to exist."

And then he said, "People like us have always existed. Here, in the desert, they call us in-betweeners. On the Coast, we say ichidi. Being genderless in the Shoal is not the same as being ichidi."

"What is the difference?" I asked him.

"The difference is that you choose."

I thought about this a lot since then. Everybody is the same in the Shoal, but Old Song chose to be a woman, as fast as she could. She gave that rebellion to me too. Not how she wanted, perhaps; but I, too, could choose—to be a woman, a man, or an in-betweener—and still be seen.

Perhaps I only dreamed all this.

I wipe my face. Tell Ulín, "You told me he is a cruel person. A person who always was hard and cold, even as a child. He judges himself as harshly. He is a loner and hated by many. You were summoned here because Ladder wants him dead."

She says, "I am not sure if I understand the Headmaster's reasons."

I shrug. "The Raker thought it was jealousy—I understood that in Che Mazri, the Raker had met and courted Ladder's old lover. Perhaps it was a different jealousy—

jealousy of the Orphan, the Ladder's second-choice star that spent five whole nights with the Raker and did not want to let him go. I am not sure. Does it matter? Ladder wants him dead, you want him dead—do you?"

Ulín does not reply.

I try again. "Why not Laufkariar? He certainly harmed you as much, if not more. Or your father. He was not a child, and yet he took your freedom from you, drugged you, dismissed you."

Ulín is silent still.

"Shall I read your paper now?" I attempt a smile, half-frustrated, half-amused. "Certainly it would be a relief for me if you finally choose a target. I will graduate and with luck, my contract will be sold, and I might even see new places."

Ulín inhales deeply. "When we study languages, we learn to hold complexity."

"How does that relate?"

She tells me, "Studying languages, I learned that nothing is ever as simple as *friend*, or *enemy*, or *powerless*, or *powerful*, or *kill*, or *forgive*. In my land, men and women and ichidar live together and do as they choose, and yet my whole life had been shaped by these three people and the harm they caused me." Her shoulders hunch, as if she is cold, even though it is never cold here. I think I understand.

I say, "You must hold this complexity now, and it must be held in your body, a body which these three people had harmed so cruelly, so thoughtlessly."

"It's not fair," she says.

"So I'll kill him at your word. Any one of *him*."

"Even my brother?"

I nod. "Yes, even the Raker."

"I thought you cared for him," Ulín says.

"I do. But I'll take the assignment. He will understand."

She reaches her hand toward me, and traces her fingers along mine. This is the first time she has initiated touch, and I do not move away. "Help me understand, Stone Orphan."

I speak my thoughts that I never voiced to anyone. "The whole world devours. Stars uphold the land, but they must absorb souls to keep living, no matter what language we use."

"I believe not all stars are like this," Ulín protests.

"Maybe, but these are the stars I know. We live under the yoke of the stars, and under the yoke of each other. We are held so tightly, first willingly, then against our will, then perhaps willingly again, but it does not matter, because we are held, inescapably held, by each other and the stars."

She smiles and pulls back. "Unroll my note, Stone Orphan, and read the name of the target."

I do so. The paper is empty.

I say, "I do not understand."

"This is what I can give you," Ulín says. "What I can give both of us. Freedom."

I still do not understand. "What does it mean to you? Freedom."

"Freedom does not have to be empty of people," she says. "This I learned from the Kran-Valadar, and from all of the stories you and I told each other. People can hold you, and yet not jail you. People can gift you their words and their stories and listen attentively to yours. People can love you and yet not constrain you. People can hate you, and yet choose to turn away from violence. Freedom is not pain, but neither is it painless; freedom is choice, even if it leads you wrong. Freedom is to seek more knowledge, even if others think that you are naïve."

Ulín exhales, and I exhale with her.

She tells me, "Today I use my freedom to say, *I cannot go through with this now. I must learn more, and think.*"

III.
TOWARD

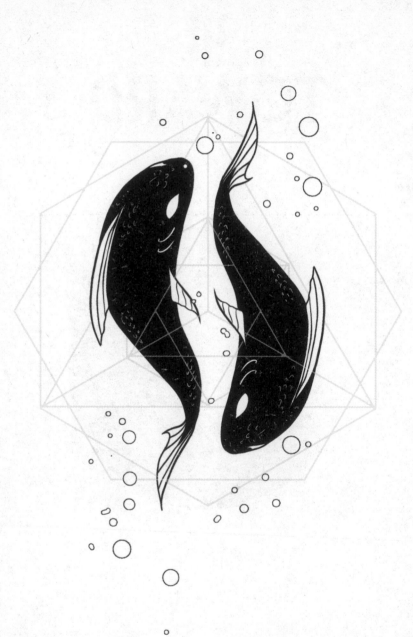

I TELL ULÍN, "I would tell you one last story. A story that does not exist."

In my story, Old Song made a new choice at last, after all her betrayals and her lies and her hurts and her hesitations. In my story, she'd chosen out of love to become bereft, and yet free.

She told me that I was brave and that she wasn't. But in my story, after I left, she made herself braver. And so she decided to translate herself away from our people and into that wood where the nameway and dreamway people of Lysinar live together under the wise and illustrious guidance of the Kran-Valadar.

"What do you want?" I had asked the Raker.

He told me, in the end. He said the same thing. "I want to be free in my ways. Neither prisoning nor prisoner. Free."

He always used to say, *Everybody wants something from me.* This was true for me, too. The Star of the Shoal wanted me to never separate from the collective, not in a breath or a dream, to be held together with them in the Shoal's own safety and fear. Ladder wanted me because he thought I had skills that could serve him and the

Orphan. I escaped my old world, but I did not deviate from this new shoal. I learned this new language, and I learned the body. I wanted to train and make progress, to follow the rules and the orders. Fulfill contracts chosen for me.

I tell Ulín, "At first, I thought what you wanted from me was the contract. Then I thought it was my language. But you wanted—you wanted to hear me, and to be heard. Is that freedom? Or is that a kind of a shoal? Could I have that with others, without coercion or fear?"

"You can," she says to me. "I think we both can."

I say, "You know, I had always waited for others to bond with me. My parent bonded with me. Then Old Song. Even Ladder, they all reached out to me with their power. But if I am to be free, I can choose."

"Who would you choose, then?" Ulín is curious now.

There is only one answer I want to give to this. "I would rebond with Old Song."

If I were to choose to bond again with Old Song, I would reach out to her with my power. I am an exile and forbidden to return to the isles, but in my story, Old Song would no longer be in the Shoal. She would be in the wood, and so she would be free to reject me or to accept me, without the laws of the Shoal.

Ulín nods at me. "You would forgive her?"

"I . . . I would want to begin again. No, I . . . I would want the story to go on."

We look at each other, and Ulín's eyes glisten.

I say, "This is painful, Ulín."

"Yes," she agrees.

Even if Song is not in the Shoal, she had wounded

me. She could have refused, but she did not dare. Is she brave enough now? Is she an orphan like me, or did she stay in the Shoal? Is she yearning? Or did she forget me? Will she understand that I am not a woman, and yet not lesser for it?

Still. If she is free and would accept me, then I would flicker toward her. I would translate myself again, from this place to be at her side, and I would retell my story once more in a language woven together of threads and of stories—neither siltway nor nameway or dreamway, neither old nor new. Something different and difficult, but still entirely mine.

I ask Ulín, "If Old Song is in the wood, and if she accepts my bond, would you travel with me?"

She is startled. "Can this even be done?"

"Oh, I think so." In fact, I am sure of it. "The two of us now share something which is very much like a bond. If you hold my hand, I will hold you with my deepnames as if you were mortar. We will travel—and not like a figure on ground, but between soul to soul, all distance swallowed by breath."

"I am not sure I understand siltway travel," Ulín says, but I worry that her hesitation is about something else.

I say, "Or you can stay here without me. Now that you won't choose your contract, you can simply leave, if Ladder allows it. You heard his song, after all, but I think you'll have choices."

"No, I—I don't understand how this will work, but I want this to work. I want to travel with you. I trust you, and . . ." Ulín laughs. "I always want to travel."

I, too, want for this to work. I want Old Song to be

in the wood, where she can reject or accept me. I want her to accept me. I want to leave the Court of Despair behind, for Ladder to solve his own problems. For the story not to end, but to go on.

Ulín is putting away her notebook. "If this doesn't work, I want you to know—we can travel my way, all the long way back to Lysinar."

I nod at her, oddly encouraged. We have exchanged yearning and pain, but we can be free together, free of the yoke of the devouring stars. Traveling—not away from, but toward.

I tell Ulín, "Hold my hand."

Neither pain nor yearning now

The room on the third terrace is empty. The shallow water in the pool is dull and lifeless. There is no need to refill it again.

AFTERWORD

Motion is central not just to human experience, but to our cognition. Even if we cannot physically walk or run, we process the world through motion metaphors. Business is hopping, time really crawls, you ran out of pasta. We do not physically sprint out of the gates of pasta, but how we talk about this is meaningful. Even when we sleep, the neurons responsible for motion are firing, producing dreams of chases and abrupt relocations.

Human languages describe motion in many ways, but most commonly through verbs; verbs are ubiquitous in human languages. How exactly motion events are coded varies, sometimes greatly, from language to language, and is a robust area in linguistic research. I've done some of this research myself. As a linguist in graduate school, I began wondering about an idea of a verbless language—the existence of such a language would imply a completely different way of moving, of thinking, and of interacting with the world. (Much later, I discovered that there is a constructed language, Kēlen, built to engage with this question—but I do not know anything else about it. I wanted to continue thinking my own thoughts.)

The idea of a verbless language compelled me to write my first short story, in which an exile ends up at the school of assassins. That first story was never published, and it's a good thing—I did not have the tools, or know my own mind back then. But the story continued to percolate in my mind. I realized I wanted to write not just about a community with a very different way of thinking, but about bilingualism. And it wasn't just about bilingualism (that is, about knowing and speaking two languages)—but about exile, about translating oneself away not just from one's culture, but from one's language and community.

Stone Orphan is an exile. They wanted to leave, and they were also kicked out. This happens to some of us. When I was fourteen, my family fled the Soviet Union during the last months of its existence, among hundreds of thousands of other Soviet Jews. As an out queer, nonbinary person born in Soviet Ukraine who came out in the U.S., I felt unrooted and disconnected from my often heteronormative diasporic and birth communities.

But while I was in the West, things evolved for both Ukraine and Russia, where I had also lived as a child. Queer and trans people gained freedoms and recognition in both countries, and both Russian and Ukrainian developed language innovations for nonbinary people. During Russia's genocidal war against Ukraine, Putin's regime cranked down on the LGBTQIA+ community, with overwhelming and total persecution of queer expression and outlawing of gender transition. My birth country, Ukraine, is perhaps moving the other way. Just a few months before writing this, my poem cycle, "Stone Listening," was translated into Ukrainian by Mykhailo Zharzhailo and published in Litcentr. My correct gender pronouns were used in the bio; just a few years ago, I would not believe it would be possible.

Diasporic and migrant experiences of LGBTQIA+ people are also a special interest of mine and a topic in my linguistic research. It's a painful thing. Migrating from country to country is difficult to begin with, but queer and trans people are often liminal—both within their birth and host communities. The new country we enter may seem welcoming at first, but that can be deceptive and temporary. Stone Orphan discovers this the hard way when they come to the school of assassins. Their sense of liberation does not last just because they migrated; but the hope for liberation persists. For a long time, the U.S. seemed like a haven to me in terms of my queerness, but now the wave of discrimination is rising again. My home state of Kansas just passed cissexist legislation that we are resisting as a community. Is any place safe? Is any place good? I don't know, but what we can find is each other.

When Ulín and Stone Orphan connect, they are speaking Burrashti, a language which both of them learned in adulthood. Both of them are translating, and both of them are hiding parts of their stories. Stone Orphan does not want to reveal everything to a person they just met, and even at the end, their friendship with Ulín is still tentative. Ulín is driven by her curiosity. She is traumatized, but through all this she is propelled forward by her special interest in languages and the people who speak them.

Language is not disembodied—it exists in communities, and it is learned and spoken by people. Both Ulín and Stone Orphan want to understand. This is the bridge they can build together, even though bridges do not always exist, or are unhelpful or inaccessible, or are destroyed. The necessity of bridges is that we cannot always flicker from one person to another; often, crossing requires difficult and careful labor. Perhaps we must meet each other first, before travel can become instantaneous.

Just before Russia's full-scale invasion of Ukraine in 2022, I was working on translation theory research—looking at how gender was translated in the works of Cold War era science fiction, from English to Russian and from Russian to English. When Russia's war against Ukraine broke out, I became involved in translating war poetry from Ukrainian to English, and had many opportunities to connect and collaborate with poets writing about their experiences of war. You can find some of these translations and many others in *Chytomo Magazine*'s English-language issues of Ukrainian war poetry. There are so many vital and necessary things yet to discover and discuss about language, and cultures, and translation. I believe that the work of translation and of linguistic research remains vital and necessary, even as technology gains traction—and minority languages continue to be endangered as hegemonic languages expand.

I am a person who can think about a single thing for

decades, turning and turning it around. I've been rotating this story in my mind for as long as I've been writing. Now you have read it—thank you. I hope you can come away from this book with my hope for the world, and for us: that we are not prisoners of our hurts, that we can be together and yet free.

Concepts and further reading:

Many ideas about the collectivist society in this book were inspired by my lived experience as an ex-Soviet person (as well as by my academic research into this history). Stone Orphan's and Old Song's judgment harkens back to Soviet-era comrades' courts.

For the concept of Figure and Ground, take a look at Leonard Talmy's theories. Talmy, L. (2000). *Towards a Cognitive Semantics, Vol. 1: Concept Structuring Systems*. Cambridge (MA), Massachusetts Institute of Technology.

For motion verbs and motion events research—begin with the work of Dan Slobin; I recommend his chapter, "The Many Ways to Search for a Frog: Linguistic Typology and the Expression of Motion Events." Slobin, D. I. (2004). In S. Strömqvist, & L. Verhoeven (eds.), *Relating Events in Narrative, Vol. 2: Typological and Contextual Perspectives* (pp. 219-257). Mahwah, NJ: Lawrence Erlbaum Associates Publishers.

There are many excellent articles and books about encoding motion events in the languages of the world: search Google Scholar for "motion events" or "motion verbs" and your language of interest.

For cognition and space, I recommend Levinson's work: Levinson, S. C. (2003). *Space in Language and Cognition: Explorations in Cognitive Diversity* (Vol. 5). Cambridge University Press.

Finally, a lot of Ulín's research and my worldbuilding reflects my special interest in etymologies and in the Nostratic theory research during the Soviet regime. Roughly speaking, the Nostratic theory postulates that the major language families of the Eurasian continent and of North Africa (the Indo-European, Afro-Asiatic, and Finno-Ugric language families, as well as other languages and language families) all had a common ancestor, the Nostratic proto-language. I find the theory itself problematic and unprovable (at least, at this stage of our knowledge and documentation), but the research done under the Soviet regime is deeply valuable. Because universities were governmentally funded and because historical linguistics research was often carried out in teams, Soviet-era scholars had unprecedented opportunities to work on topics which are perceived as "useless" and not "commercially viable" in the Western academy. These scholars include Soviet Jewish historical linguists V.M. Illich-Svitych and Aharon Dolgopolsky, both of whom worked on Nostratic theory and dictionaries. Dolgopolsky taught at first at the Moscow State University and then in Haifa University, and his monumental *Nostratic Dictionary* was published by Cambridge University Press in 2008. You can download a free pdf from Cambridge: https://core.ac.uk/download/pdf/1302376.pdf

I've spent a lot of time with this book, looking at Dolgopolsky's endless and massive word comparisons (again, this is a special interest, the core of my own research is elsewhere). You see some of this reflected in just a single word that appears in the book. Dolgopolsky reconstructs *kälû as a Nostratic word for woman, or more precisely a woman of the opposite exogamous moiety within an exogamic cultural system. This is reflected in geographically far-flung languages such as Semitic kall-at- 'bride,' Old Georgian kal-i 'daughter, maid,' Finnish käly 'sister-in-law,' and many others (Dolgopolsky 2008: 817-818).

In a different, yet to be published fantasy book of mine, Ulín proposes a unity of dreamway languages, which later comes to be disproven—but the research is still meaningful. This is my overarching take on Nostratic theory. We arrive at knowledge despite past and ongoing injustices of political systems, and the failures and controversies around the conclusions we might reach. Our processes may be flawed and the conclusions may be wrong, but the words and connections are there.

ACKNOWLEDGEMENTS

Thank you to the early readers of my stories: Kathryn Schild, Shweta Narayan, Jonathan Cohen, and Diana Dima. Shweta, thank you for telling me that I should write (this, and other things). Kathryn, thank you for telling me that this was good. It's a very different story now and I'm a very different person now, but this is also still the same. Jonathan and Diana, thank you for finding value and meaning in my early work, before I trusted or knew myself.

Thank you to all the Birdverse readers over the years, to my wonderful Patreon subscribers who have supported my work for so long. Many thanks to my publishing team—my incredible editor Jaymee Goh, who gets my work so deeply. To my agent Mary C. Moore, for her hard work on my behalf; to Jacob Weisman, Jill Roberts, Kasey Lansdale, Rick Klaw, Elizabeth Story, and Anne Zanoni. I am so happy to work with you all.

Thank you above all to Bogi Takács ☺ After toward came together.

To A.: I am sorry I could not do better, faster, and

more decisively. I don't know if this breath will ever be sovereign, but if and when it will prevail, you'll be the first to know.

Le Guin Feminist Fellow **R. B. Lemberg** is a queer, bigender fantasist, poet, and professor originally from L'viv, Ukraine.

R. B.'s first Birdverse novella *The Four Profound Weaves* (Tachyon) was a finalist for the Nebula, Ignyte, Locus, and World Fantasy awards. Their second Birdverse book from Tachyon, *The Unbalancing,* was selected for many best books of the year lists such as the *Washington Post, Lit Hub, Book Riot,* and *Autostraddle.* R. B.'s first short fiction collection, *Geometries of Belonging* (Fairwood Press) came out in 2022 and was a finalist for the 2023 Ursula K. Le Guin Prize for Fiction. Their poetry memoir *Everything Thaws* (Ben Yehuda Press) came out in 2023. Their stories and poems have appeared in *Lightspeed Magazine's Queers Destroy Science Fiction!, Beneath Ceaseless Skies, We Are Here: Best*

Queer Speculative Fiction 2020, Sisters of the Revolution: A Feminist Speculative Fiction Anthology, and many other venues.

R. B. lives in Lawrence, Kansas, with their spouse and fellow author Bogi Takács, their child Mati, and all of the cumulative books and fountain pens. You can find R. B. on Instagram at @rblemberg,, on Patreon at patreon.com/rblemberg, and at their website rblemberg.net.